SAMUEL

TEARS

OF A

NATION

Books by Daniel Drazen
Samuel: One Small Light

To order, call 1-800-765-6955.

Visit us at www.reviewandherald.com for information on other
Review and Herald products.

SAMUEL

T E A R S

O F   A

N A T I O N

Daniel J. Drazen

REVIEW AND HERALD® PUBLISHING ASSOCIATION
HAGERSTOWN, MD 21740

The author assumes full responsibility for the accuracy of all facts and quotations as cited in this book.

This book was
Edited by Gerald Wheeler
Design by O'Connor Creative
Cover photo by Joel D. Springer
Typeset: 12/14 Bembo

PRINTED IN U.S.A.

08 07 06 05 04   5 4 3 2 1

R&H Cataloging Service
Drazen, Daniel Joseph, 1951–
    Samuel: tears of a nation.

    1. Samuel (Biblical judge).   I. Title.

            221.92

ISBN 0-8280-1774-3

Dedicated

to
the memory
of
my parents

Part One

HANNAH AWOKE TO THE SOUND of crying. When she opened her eyes it was still night.

The only light came from a small clay oil lamp flickering on a shelf against the far wall. In its dim illumination she could see the indistinct shapes of her two daughters, Elisheba and Jedidah, sleeping on the floor of their room. She could also hear someone stirring and muttering in the adjoining room where her husband's other wife, Peninah, slept with her daughter, Lebiya. Her husband, Elkanah, occupied a third room with his older sons.

Picking up Ahitub, the child lying near her, Hannah rose, and holding him to her bosom with one arm, threaded her way around the others as she walked to the door. Lifting the latch, she stepped outside into the clear, cold night.

The barley harvest was over, and the harvest of wheat would soon start. While the days steadily grew warmer, the cloudless nights could still be bitterly cold. It was almost the beginning of the month, so there was no moon. Hannah wrapped another layer of cloak around the baby, which also muffled his crying. She felt him writhe and snuggle closer to her warmth, trying to escape the chill.

As her eyes adjusted to the starlight, she saw a shadow by the entrance to their courtyard. Approaching closer, she could see that it was her son, Samuel, recently returned to their home in Ramah. He sat with his back against the wall, his knees drawn up and his arms resting upon them, staring up into the night sky.

"Samuel?"

Hannah knew he wasn't asleep, only preoccupied. She'd noticed it several times since his return. He glanced toward her.

"Mother, is something wrong with him?" he asked in a half-whisper.

"Just hungry," she said in the matter-of-fact way of women who have raised more than one child and for whom nothing is an emergency or a surprise anymore.

"Oh." Samuel went back to looking at the night sky.

"Did you have another dream?"

"No," he said, shaking his head. "I . . . I just couldn't go to sleep." For a moment he rubbed his eyes with one hand. "We were two nights in the fields during the lambing."

"You'll get used to it," she said as reassuringly as possible.

"Sometimes . . . sometimes I don't think I'll ever get used to *any* of it!" he answered, his voice rising slightly. "As far back as I can remember I've been . . ."

"Helping Eli?"

With a nod he bowed his head. "I know I was doing what the Lord meant for me to do back then, but . . . but now I'm afraid I'm not good for anything anymore."

"Samuel," she said with just enough firmness in her voice to catch his attention, "how much do you think this little one knows about farming?"

"About as much as I do," he sighed.

"Then you'll learn together."

"Mother, I . . . I know the Lord meant me to do something for Him. I've heard it all my life. I even *heard* His voice at the sanctuary! But back there I thought I understood what He wanted of me. Now I don't." He paused to run the back of one hand across his eyes.

"Did you understand it when you got there?"

His head still bowed, Samuel said nothing.

"Did you understand it?"

"No," he admitted with another sigh. "I had to learn."

"And now you have to learn all over again. That can be pretty hard to accept."

"Especially when Shemed and Izhar won't let me forget it," he said, referring to Peninah's two oldest sons.

"I know that can be hard, too."

Samuel dried his eyes once more. He turned to face his mother. "What should I do?"

"Just do what you're doing now: continue to learn, continue trying, and continue trusting."

"I will," he said in the darkness.

"Now go inside—it's too cold to be out."

"Not yet. I want to watch the stars a while longer."

"Why?"

"Looking at them reminds me of home—of the tabernacle," he quickly added.

Hannah didn't say anything. Sensing that the infant in her arms had dropped back to sleep, she turned back to the house. "Just don't stay out too long."

"I won't."

Hannah returned to the house, and Samuel resumed staring up at the stars. Even if the stars embroidered on the ceiling of the tabernacle had only been a faint imitation of the evening sky, it was still something familiar, something reminiscent. Samuel knew that he had hurt Hannah's feelings by referring to the tabernacle as "home," but he couldn't help it—that was what it *felt* like.

★　★　★

Elkanah's farm was well-to-do by the standards of Ramah. Because his family was so large, what with having children first by Peninah and then by Hannah, he had needed to add two more rooms to the standard four-room Israelite house plan. Ordinarily, the front area would be used to take meals and to entertain while the rear was private space for sleeping. It wasn't much different from the old nomadic life of their ancestors, he told himself. It was just like dividing a large tent into extra rooms using curtains.

Not even a year ago 12 people had shared the home: Elkanah, his two wives, and his nine children, four by Hannah and five by Peninah. Some of the people on neighboring farmsteads, who didn't know any better, called the extended family a blessing. Elkanah knew that it was a nightmare.

He had fully intended to live his life married to only one woman—

Hannah. But when it had become clear that she was barren Elkanah had reluctantly accepted the idea of taking a second wife. "After all," he told himself, "our fathers Abraham and Jacob did the same." Hard as he tried, though, he could think of no other good reason.

Peninah had borne him four sons and a daughter: Shemed, Izhar, Zaccur, Manoah, and finally Helah. The other men jested that Peninah had actually given birth to eight sons, with Helah acting like four boys all by herself. Perhaps it was because she grew up with so many brothers, but even from a young age she had had little patience for cooking, weaving, and other domestic arts. While she learned them well enough, still she was always ready to drop them at a moment's notice to help with the work of the farm or, more often than not, to avenge herself for a teasing remark from one of the brothers by showering blows like hailstones on him. That had quickly earned her the nickname Lebiya, the "fierce lioness," from her brothers. If they had meant it to shame her, it didn't work. After a time she would respond to no other name.

It was how things would have remained had not Hannah, for whom Elkanah clearly had more affection than for Peninah, finally (and many said miraculously) conceived and bore Samuel. Even this didn't bother the brothers so much, especially when they realized that Hannah planned to take Samuel to Shiloh and leave him in the care of the high priest. None of them had ever seen Eli, but they had heard that he was as foolish as he was old.

Peninah and her children were mistaken in thinking that Samuel's departure from the home would put things back the way they had been before. Hannah bore four more children after that—two sons and two daughters. That led to a precarious balance. Peninah begrudged it as deeply as Hagar had resented having to vie with Sarah for the affections of Abraham. The children of Elkanah's second wife had to content themselves with the fact that Hannah's children, being younger, were easier to bully when nobody was watching.

Like any truce, it took at least as much effort to make it work as it would have required to go to war. The extended family silently negotiated and strictly enforced living arrangements. Peninah's children, however, made it a point to keep their distance from their father's children by Hannah at every opportunity, even if it meant doing extra work in the field or tending the herd of goats that they kept. It pained Elkanah to think that it was the price he had to pay for his seeming prosperity.

Elkanah remembered when it had all come crashing down five months ago. That day he had been at work in his fields with his children by Peninah. Those by Hannah were either too young or else helping prepare the day's food. It was the time of the olive harvest. He had just emptied another basket of olives into the stone trough that doubled as a winepress during the grape harvest. Wiping the sweat from his brow and looking up from his work, he had seen someone approaching along the road. The traveler carried one sack slung across his back and held something else against his chest. *Another refugee,* he thought. *What else could it be? One more poor soul seeking shelter from the Sea People.*

But Elkanah's brow furrowed as he kept looking. There was something unusual about this traveler and his slow, plodding step, putting one foot in front of the other as dully as an ox. Then he realized what it was: it was the clothes he was wearing. Although torn and covered with dirt, they were made of white linen.

Letting the woven basket drop from his hand to the ground, Elkanah began to walk, then run, toward the road where the person now stood. Just then the refugee allowed the sack slung over one shoulder to fall behind him. But he clung to the object in his arms. By the time Elkanah reached the edge of his field at a full run, his heart was beating so fast that he could hear its pounding. When he reached the road, he came to a dead stop. Standing there in front of him, wearing the white linen of the priesthood, looking as if he had witnessed a hundred tragedies, swayed his son Samuel. The boy looked at his father and tried to speak, but no words escaped his mouth. Then he collapsed to the ground, still clinging to the burden in his arms.

For two nights and a day Samuel was little more than conscious. At times he would lie awake, eyes open, saying nothing, asking nothing. Every time Elkanah thought he was about to speak the boy would turn his face toward the wall and stare at it, his expression blank.

"What's everyone so concerned about?" Shemed sniffed as the

sons of Peninah gathered by themselves to share the evening meal. "It's easy to see what's going on. The seer's come home with his tail between his legs, and now he thinks he's too good to work alongside the rest of us."

The others nodded.

"Does anyone know *what* happened at the sanctuary?" Zaccur asked.

"Nothing that any two people I've spoken to can agree on," Izhar replied.

"I get the impression that it was bad, whatever it was," Shemed muttered.

"It doesn't matter to me what happened, so long as he starts pulling his share of the weight," Zaccur added.

"Probably hasn't done a day's *real* work in his life, and we'll be expected to teach him," Izhar said.

"I'm not looking forward to that," Shemed growled.

The following day Samuel rose from where he had been lying. When Elkanah and Hannah asked how he was feeling, he insisted that he wanted to help out around the farmstead. Hannah had her doubts. His assurances that he was all right seemed flat and lifeless— as if he only half-believed them himself—but she didn't say anything. She was glad enough to see him making the effort to become part of farm life, and since the arrival of Ahitub had coincided with that of Samuel, she definitely had other things on her mind.

As it was the time of the olive harvest, Elkanah sent Samuel and Lebiya, along with his sons by Peninah, to harvest the remaining olives from the half-dozen trees that grew on the land. Borrowing a shepherd's staff, Samuel walked after the older boys, who pointedly ignored him. Lebiya, who was carrying six woven baskets nested inside one another, didn't try to make conversation either.

It didn't take the brothers long to let Samuel know his status on the farm. They had been harvesting the olives for some time. The procedure was simple enough. Using long poles or shepherd staffs, they knocked the branches of the trees, causing the olives to rain to the ground where the baskets caught as many as possible. Afterward, they hand-gathered those that had landed outside the baskets and took everything to the oil press.

Samuel worked quietly, not even making any effort to speak to his half brothers, which suited them just fine. They were gratified to notice, though, that he flinched as the olives pelted down on him. When Shemed and Izhar exchanged glances, Shemed nodded and backed up slowly until he stood just out of sight behind Samuel. Raising his staff again to strike a nearby branch, Samuel was in mid-swing when Shemed swept his pole and deftly struck the backs of Samuel's knees. Caught off balance, the boy lost his balance and fell backward. The brothers laughed heartily. As he pulled himself to his feet, about a dozen olives still stuck on Samuel's back.

"That's not how you press olives!" Izhar laughed.

"Hey, seer!" Zaccur called out. "How come you couldn't fore-see that?"

"Ignore them," Lebiya said half aloud as she brushed the olives from Samuel's back onto the ground, then quickly scooped them into a nearby basket and handed it to him. Taking another basket, she started back toward the house with Samuel following her. Lebiya waited until the sound of laughter had faded.

"There are two things you need to remember about them," she said as they walked, though she never looked directly at him. "The first thing is, they're all fools."

"And the second thing?"

"Never forget the first thing."

Samuel smiled and almost laughed.

"We never went to the sanctuary," she went on. "Mother al-ways came up with some reason for her and us not to go, and Father always gave in. That's why he only took Hannah and her children after a while. I've always wondered—what is it like?"

When Samuel didn't reply, Lebiya paused and turned around.

He was about 30 paces behind her, standing still and staring off into space. His arms hung down, allowing the basket to tip and drib-ble olives onto the ground.

"Samuel?"

She hurried over to him. He was so stiff and so still that he could have been dead, but his eyes were open. Something about those eyes unsettled her. They appeared to be fixed on a point a good way above the horizon, as if he was watching a nonexistent cloud. When she tried to take the basket from him, he continued to cling to it.

"What's the matter with the seer?" Zaccur asked as he walked up, his stick resting on one shoulder. "Is he tired out already?"

"I think there's something wrong with him."

"Nothing that getting his mind back on his work won't cure," Shemed said as he took hold of the basket and tried to wrench it from Samuel's grip. It wouldn't budge. After two tries, Shemed let go and backed away.

"Now who's slacking off from work?" Lebiya taunted, then quickly ducked out of the way before getting slapped for her insolence.

"What's going on?" Elkanah asked as he approached, his concern clearly visible on his face.

"Something's wrong with Samuel," Lebiya replied. "He's acting unusual."

"He's acting crazy," Izhar added.

"Quiet, both of you," Elkanah said as he warily paced around Samuel.

"What are you looking for?" Shemed asked, clearly not interested in any kind of answer.

"I've seen this look before. Sometimes Hannah would be this way. It wouldn't last that long, though. Afterward she'd tell me about things she'd seen."

Just then the basket slipped from Samuel's grasp and dropped to the ground. He would have collapsed to the ground as well had not Elkanah caught him by the shoulders. "Samuel!" he said, shaking him for good measure. "Samuel! Can you hear me?"

For a moment the boy's expression remained blank, then he looked from Elkanah to Lebiya and back to Elkanah. It was as if he were seeing them for the first time and didn't know who they were. Then, just as quickly, he blinked, and a look of recognition crept into his eyes.

"Samuel! Are you all right?" Elkanah asked.

"I . . . I think so."

"Did you . . . see anything?"

"I can't remember."

"It's all right. Go inside and rest."

"And leave us to do his work!" Shemed snapped.

"Enough! You get back to the trees."

Shemed's brow furrowed as he walked briskly away.

Elkanah then returned his attention to Samuel. "Can you walk?"

"Yes," he replied, but doubt echoed in his voice as he said it.

"Lebiya, take him to the house—make sure he gets there all right."

"I'm fine!" Samuel protested.

"Let's go," Lebiya said as she advanced two steps ahead, then stopped, expecting him to follow her. He glanced at Elkanah, then joined Lebiya. They continued in silence for about 30 heartbeats before Samuel said, without any kind of prompting, "Mice."

"What?" she asked.

"I saw mice."

★   ★   ★

It was all supposed to be so familiar, yet it was all so strange. Even eating.

Especially during mealtimes Samuel realized just how alien his life had been at the sanctuary. While there he had eaten the customary two meals of the day—the first after the morning sacrifice and the other after the evening sacrifice—and he had thought the food there to be perfectly ordinary.

Now he knew better. The food that he had shared with Eli, though simple, had been of high quality. The bread of the presence, which the high priest had allowed Samuel to share along with the other priests (whatever their reservations about it), was lighter both in texture and in color. The vegetable stews were heady with such spices as coriander and cumin.

Then he received extra food between meals. Because fire did not consume the peace offerings (as was the case with the sin offerings), it was customary for the worshiper and his family to share their portion with Eli, which meant with Samuel as well. As a result the boy dined fairly regularly on dishes containing ox or goat meat. So did Eli. Small wonder, Samuel told himself, that the high priest had become obese.

Here it was all different—not only the food itself but the *feeling* as well. At the sanctuary Samuel had always dined with Eli apart from the other priests. Eli's own sons, Hophni and Phinehas, especially made it a point to avoid their father's presence whenever possible. It could sometimes get lonely when he was eating with Eli, particularly when the high priest slipped into one of his darker moods. At those times the boy was glad to be able to take a dish of food over to Issachar. Issachar was a Levite who had been born blind. The tribe was under obligation to care for him as he was ritually unable to perform the work of a priest, but nobody seemed to have figured out what exactly to do with him. So he was left alone, nursing a bitterness against the world. Even after encountering Samuel and eventually demonstrating a skill at the potter's wheel, he could be gruff and abusive. Still, the boy never felt that the man was being cruel when he'd ask him awkward or provocative questions during their conversations.

Now, however, Samuel was sharing food with an entire family—his own family—and he'd simply had no preparation for such an experience. Elkanah was, of course, at the center of things, and the women always laid out the food before him to bless. His sons by Peninah, who spoke only to each other during the meals, always formed a tight circle around him. The family regarded Lebiya and the children of Hannah as being too young to sit with the men, so they would eat with their mothers. Even here, though, Samuel sensed something wrong. Peninah ate apart from Hannah, not even looking at her, while Hannah found herself kept busy even after the work of meal preparation trying to control Samuel's younger siblings. They ranged in age from 7-year-old Allon to the newborn Ahitub. Lebiya never offered to help Hannah and didn't even speak to her.

As for Samuel, they considered him old enough to eat with Elkanah and his half brothers, but he may as well have been invisible as far as the older boys were concerned. They would either concentrate on their food, which they ate with more noise than necessary whenever Samuel tried to say something, or else conversed among themselves.

And then there was the food itself. The stews were blander and the bread coarser and heavier. And it had to be stretched to feed another mouth. When 5-year-old Gershom tactlessly remarked on the skimpy quantity to his mother, Hannah, Samuel saw her sigh and shake her head as if to say: "With so many to feed, this is the best I can do." He also saw Peninah and Shemed glance at her. Samuel guessed that they wanted to tell her: "If you'd rather we have fewer mouths to feed, we know where to start."

Some of this, such as the separation of the men from the women and children, was the normal custom, the way that it had been done for generations. The men conversed among themselves, and no one made any effort to interrupt them. And nobody expected that to change.

Lebiya, however, seemed to have other ideas. Glancing up from her food into Samuel's face, she said in a voice loud enough to make sure Elkanah and the men heard her: "Samuel, what was that you said earlier about mice?"

The men instantly lapsed into silence.

"Mice?" Elkanah asked. "Who said anything about mice?"

"Samuel did. Remember when you came over from the fields to see if he was all right? We'd been taking the olives back to the house when he stopped and just kept staring across the fields. When I took him home, he said something about seeing mice."

"He meant that he'd seen your face!" Izhar piped up, as he squinted his eyes and wrinkled his nose at Lebiya. The other brothers burst out laughing.

"Let's see what you look like with a sandal in your mouth!"

"Stop it! Right now!" Elkanah shouted. "Samuel, what did you mean by that?"

"He didn't mean anything," Shemed interrupted. "That's just his way of getting out of work."

"Well, if the Lord sent him a warning that our fields are going to be overrun by mice, I'd like to know that!"

"No, it wasn't our field," Samuel said with some hesitation as he furrowed his brow and tried to remember what he had seen. "It was a field, but it wasn't ours. It looked different"

"What, did the wheat grow upside down?"

"I'm warning you, Izhar! Go on, Samuel."

"It was a wheat field like ours, but the edges, the background . . ."

"The horizon?" Lebiya asked.

"The horizon . . . it was flatter—no hills like around here. And I noticed a city beyond the field. I'd recognize it if I saw it again."

"But what about the mice?" Elkanah persisted.

"They were in the field, thousands of them, devouring the crops. And I could hear many voices coming from the city, wailing in sorrow because of the mice."

"I know what comes next," Izhar declared. "Then the mice all get eaten by seven hungry cows!"

"I told you to be quiet!" Elkanah shouted.

"Father, we've heard stories like this all our lives. It's just too bad Samuel didn't learn anything more useful at the sanctuary than storytelling."

"It's not a story! I *saw* it!"

"That's enough out of all of you! As for Samuel . . ."

But the boy had risen from where he was seated in the main room of the house and practically run outside, across the courtyard, and into the gathering twilight.

"Samuel!" Hannah called after him.

"Let me get him," Lebiya said. Then turning to face her brothers, she added, "The air's getting too stale in here anyway."

Before any of them could think of a retort, she followed Samuel outside. He had stopped not 30 cubits from the house. Now he just stood there, his gaze fixed on the ground, his arms wrapped around himself as if to ward off harm or to keep himself warm. Lebiya walked up to him.

"I warned you about them." She grimaced. "I don't know which one is the biggest fool—I think they take turns."

Samuel said nothing.

"Are you all right?"

"I don't know."

"Look, they're convinced that you're not a seer, but if you saw what you did . . ."

"That's the problem," he said as he turned to face her. The sun had already set below the hills, and in the failing daylight she could see a pleading, desperate expression in his eyes. "I saw the mice as plain as day, and the city in the background, but . . ."

"But what?"

"It's what you said about the sanctuary. I can remember that as well, but . . ."

"What is it?" she asked, clearly worried.

"I remember, but I don't *want* to!"

"Was it that bad?"

Samuel nodded. "The first time God spoke to me, He told me about the death of Eli, someone who was like a father to me. And now what do I see?" he asked bitterly. "Mice!"

"Samuel, I don't know a lot about the Lord—not as much as you and Hannah seem to, anyway. What do you think it means?"

"I don't know. I'm a little afraid to find out. I still remember Eli's expression when I told him what the Lord had said to me about him and his sons and his household. I didn't want to tell him, but he wouldn't stop asking me. And then he looked as if he wished I hadn't told him." The boy pulled up a stalk of wheat, twisted it around his fingers, then dropped it back to the ground. "That's how I felt, too."

"Come on, let's get back inside. It's getting dark."

Reluctantly he silently followed her back to the house.

★　★　★

Now that he was back on his father's farm in Ramah, Samuel wanted only peace. And the Lord obliged him. Most days nothing out of the ordinary happened, no vision intruded upon his mind, and it was easy to forget who and what he was.

The day after seeing the vision of the mice promised to be just such a day. The olive harvest had yielded a good crop. But olives were valuable only because of their oil. Among many other things, his people used it to prepare food, to dress the hair, to soothe burns and wounds, and as fuel for lamps. Yet they could not obtain this blessing from the Lord simply by gathering it from the ground, as their ancestors had done the manna during the Exodus. It took work to extract the valuable oil.

"Did you have olive trees at the sanctuary?" Lebiya asked Samuel as they each carried a full basket of olives.

"Yes. We made our own oil. But we never waited this long,

though. Instead we picked them when they weren't this ripe, then pounded them with a stone."

"You must not have gotten that much."

"We got enough, even after pouring it from one jar to another again and again to make sure it was pure."

"It's about time you two got here!" Shemed scolded as they arrived at the stone trough. "You two get to work while I help the others set up the press." As he left, Lebiya set down her basket, picked out an olive, and threw it at him. Her aim was good, but it still fell short of its intended target.

"Come on," she sighed as she emptied the rest of the olives into the trough. Samuel did the same, and with Lebiya at one end and Samuel at the other, they began treading the olives, crushing them and releasing the oil.

"What did he mean by 'the press'?" Samuel asked.

"Didn't you press olives at the sanctuary?"

"No; we just used the beaten oil."

"It's a way of squeezing out the oil that's still left in the pulp after this part's done. We need to get as much as we can."

"Why?"

Lebiya paused. "We need this crop badly. Not just for ourselves, but to sell."

"I thought that the farm and the land were ours."

"So are the debts that come from working it. We've been able to feed ourselves this past year, but just barely. We've had to get help from Nehum every now and then."

"Who's he?"

"He owns a neighboring farmstead, and it's no secret he wouldn't mind adding father's holdings to his own. You'll probably see him at the house tomorrow."

"Why? What's tomorrow?"

"You don't know? Father's holding a feast in honor of Jedidah's being weaned. It took long enough; she's almost 3 years old. But I guess Hannah has nothing to celebrate, since now she's nursing Ahitub."

Ahitub! Samuel froze.

"What's the matter?"

"I . . . I just remembered something."

"About the sanctuary?"

"No, about Ahitub."

"What?"

"It's not your concern," he said as he went back to treading the olives. Lebiya glanced at the thick liquid that started to seep out from the trough into a clay jug placed beneath.

"Fine! Don't tell me! Just keep your eye on that jug and let me know when it's almost full so I can replace it."

"So what are you two old women gossiping about?" Izhar asked as he went past.

Lebiya bent down and scooped up a handful of crushed olives. "How'd you like a face full of this?"

Ignoring his sister, Izhar emptied another basket full of olives into the trough. With a look of disgust, Lebiya tossed the olives back into the trough and resumed treading the mass of olives and pulp. She watched as her brother walked away.

"I will be so glad when I don't have to answer to him anymore."

"It is that bad here?" Samuel asked.

"No, I guess not. Some have it worse," she admitted. "And I wouldn't want to live anywhere near the coast now, what with the Sea People on the move. It's just . . . there are times that I just get sick of this place, you know?"

"No, I don't," he said. "I'm still trying to get used to the idea that this is my home!"

"Well, then, you better smash this pulp as hard as you can. One or two bad harvests in a row, and this won't be anybody's home, except maybe Nehum's."

By midday Samuel and Lebiya were tired and footsore, olive pulp filled the trough, and they had collected a number of jars of oil.

"It looks like a good yield to me," Samuel observed. "And we can expect more from the pressing, right?"

"I guess so." She frowned. "I must be used to expecting the worst. Guess it comes from having to look at my brothers every day."

"I heard that!" Shemed said as he and his brothers approached.

"I *wanted* you to!"

"Here," he said as he dropped several woven baskets by the

trough. "You two shovel what's left into here, then take them to the press. We'll take care of them after the midday rest."

"Why can't we take care of this later?"

"Because I'm telling you to do it *now!* And where do you think *you're* going?" he called to Samuel, who had started toward the house.

"There's something that I need to take care of."

"Well, you can take care of this first."

Samuel opened his mouth as if to say something, then paused. "Let's get to work," he said as he picked up a basket and began scooping the remains of the olives into it by hand.

"That's better," Shemed muttered as he and the others returned to the house.

"What was that all about?" Lebiya sputtered, her fists clenched. "You let them order you around like . . ."

"Let it go. Besides, I'd just as soon take care of what I need to when they're asleep."

Snorting in disgust, Lebiya took a basket and started filling it herself. "So, just what is it that you have to do?"

Samuel glanced at her. "How do you feel about the sight of blood?"

"Doesn't scare me!" she said, drawing herself up to her full height.

"I hope not." Then, without another word, he went back to scooping.

When they finished, they brought their baskets of crushed olives to a spot in the field where a large stone outcropping stood. A niche had been cut into the stone and one end of a long wooden beam inserted into it. Underneath it was another stone trough. Samuel and Lebiya piled their baskets in the hollowed-out space.

"How does this work?" Samuel asked.

"We stack the baskets here, one on top of another. The beam goes across the top of the pile. Then they use ropes to hang those stones over there on the far end. That'll squeeze the last drops of oil out of this stuff," she added as she kicked at the baskets with her oily foot. Since the beam now rested atop it, the stack didn't move.

The two returned to the house to find that almost everyone had gone inside to take their midday nap. Hannah, however, was still sitting in the courtyard, stirring a mixture of flour and water into a dough.

"Mother," Samuel said as he entered, "where's Ahitub?"

She glanced up. "Inside. He should be asleep. Why?"

"Well, he *is* eight days old today."

Hannah stared blankly at him for a moment, then understood what he meant. "You'd better talk to your father about this."

"I will."

"Are you sure you want to do it this way?"

"Yes, Mother, I'm sure."

Standing up, she dusted off her clothes. Then she disappeared into the house, emerging a few seconds later carrying a piece of flint chipped into the shape of a knife. She handed it to him, then followed him as he went inside, with Lebiya close behind.

As Lebiya waited in the doorway, Samuel and Hannah conversed with Elkanah for a minute in his room in the back. She couldn't make out what they said and didn't dare intrude on their conversation. But she did catch Elkanah's comment, "If you feel this is right." Suddenly she started to feel uncomfortable, as if maybe she really didn't want to get involved in whatever was about to happen. But although she did step back outside, she still paused and listened by the doorway. It wasn't long before she could hear the sound of cloth ripping somewhere inside the house. Overwhelmed by curiosity, she returned inside.

Samuel held a strip of linen cloth that he had torn from the garment he had worn at the sanctuary. He set it aside on a mat where he had also put a small clay bottle of olive oil that was practically empty. The olive harvest had come just in time. Hannah emerged from her room, carrying the infant Ahitub.

"So what are you going to do?" Lebiya asked Samuel.

In answer, he took the child in his arms, then seated himself on the floor. Lebiya sat nearby as Hannah stood, watching. Carefully, Samuel unwrapped Ahitub until the infant lay naked on his lap.

Realizing what was going to happen, Lebiya solemnly took hold of the baby's legs, stretching them out. As Samuel held the knife in one hand, he took hold of the tip of the infant's foreskin between his thumb and forefinger. Then, with the swiftness of someone trimming back a grapevine, Samuel made the cut.

It took a few moments for what had happened to register with

Ahitub. By that time, Samuel had dressed the wound with the oil-soaked linen, swaddled the child once again, and handed him back to Hannah to nurse. The child was just starting to cry when Samuel rose and walked to the door, Lebiya following after.

She found him standing in the center of the courtyard, an object of curiosity for the flock of goats penned against one wall. He leaned forward with his hands on his knees, breathing heavily.

"Are you all right?" she asked.

Samuel nodded, and she waited for his breathing to return to normal.

"It's funny," he said after a minute. "I must have watched 10,000 animals die in all the time I was at the sanctuary, but this is the first time I almost fainted."

"Did you kill any of those animals?"

"No."

"Well, that's it, then. This is the first time you've shed blood, and it wasn't the blood of an animal, either. I probably would have felt the same way if I'd had to do it."

She turned back toward the house. "You coming in to rest, or are you going to stay out here?"

He straightened, then followed her toward the house.

"Look at it this way," she said as they neared the door, "now that you've shed blood, you'll be used to it when we have to start fighting the Sea People."

"Who said anything about fighting the Sea People?"

"You just wait. I'll bet you that's all the men will want to talk about at the party tonight."

★   ★   ★

Even more than their common religion, hospitality knit the Israelites in their settlement of Canaan. Everyone might spend their days preoccupied with scratching a living from their sparse farms in the rugged central highlands or moving their herds and flocks from place to place, but the feasts and celebrations allowed them to exchange hard work for a light heart.

Though Lebiya had spoken of the party as scheduled for that

night, it was more accurate to say that it took place late in the after-noon, after the midday rest and coinciding with the evening meal. That was when the guests began to arrive.

In the hours beforehand Peninah supervised the last-minute gathering of food and the placing of mats in the front room to ac-commodate the guests. She did it swiftly and efficiently, but the way she supervised Lebiya and his full sister Elisheba while refraining from doing any work herself somehow unsettled Samuel. She watched everything and everyone like some kind of predatory bird, her head thrust forward. To Samuel it looked as if she was peering over a low wall, gazing at something interesting that was actually none of her business.

Everything was in readiness as the first guests began to arrive. That is to say, it was ready to Hannah's satisfaction if not Peninah's. It was clear to Samuel that while his mother took the arrangements as seriously as Peninah did, she was also less ready to snap at the girls than her husband's other wife.

At the tabernacle the priests pretty much offered the sacrifices on their own. Eli, even before Samuel learned of his incipient blindness, did nothing to supervise them in their duties. Here, however, su-pervision seemed to be what Peninah did best. And Hannah, though aware of her own status as first wife, took it in stride. By a subtle se-ries of nods, winks, or waves of her hand she indicated to the girls which tasks they should concentrate on and which ones could wait. Samuel was pleased to see that Lebiya and Hannah worked so well together, and he began to wonder whether Lebiya's resentment of his mother and her children wasn't an act, something she did for the benefit of Peninah and her sons.

But Samuel had no time to wonder about it. His immediate task was to take a large jug to the well, fill it, and to stand near a basin in the courtyard ready to wash the feet of the guests as they arrived. This, Samuel knew, was the most common courtesy a host could ex-tend to a guest, and to neglect it represented a serious breach of eti-quette. The priests at the sanctuary washed their own feet as well as their hands to render themselves ritually clean after a sacrifice or after using the latrine. The only thing about the present situation that struck Samuel as being unusual was the fact that he had been assigned to wash the feet of others, when at the sanctuary he'd never washed anyone else's feet but his own.

The guests began arriving in pairs and small groups. Samuel gathered from their conversation that with the Sea People occupying the coastal plain, people felt it simply unwise to travel alone. He dutifully washed the feet of those who arrived. Some of them stopped to exchange a word or two with the boy; others acted as if he wasn't even there. But Samuel didn't mind. As long as he was outside in the courtyard, it meant that he wasn't available for Peninah to order about.

When the sun had dropped low in the sky and Elkanah was finally able to get away from his guests to summon Samuel to join them, the singing and dancing had already started. Someone had asked Lebiya to dance as the men and women guests sang out a tune and kept time by clapping their hands. Samuel thought that she danced the way she cleaned when her mother told her to: she went through the motions, but it was clear she had no heart for what she was doing, and she was glad to stop and to resume serving the guests. That didn't seem to matter to the guests, however.

"Thank you, my dear," Nehum said as Lebiya refilled his wine bowl. She soon lost count of the times she had already done so, and it was fairly obvious that he wasn't keeping track, either. His round face became more flushed as the party went on. Before long she was told to switch to a weaker kind of wine made by diluting the syrup prepared from boiled-down grape juice. Lebiya was certain that nobody could get intoxicated from what she was now serving, since it had been watered down so much, but Nehum didn't seem to notice. Either that or else he simply didn't care what he ate and drank so long as he didn't have to pay for it.

"Elkanah," he said as he turned toward his host, opening his arms wide as if to embrace everyone in the room at once, "you don't do anything by halves, do you?"

"I don't know what you mean," Elkanah said, and he truly meant it.

"You planned this to celebrate the weaning of one child, and you have so much else to celebrate as well: the birth of another child, the return of your son"—he nodded at Samuel, who sat at the outer edge of the circle of men, his arms held tightly against himself as if cold—"and, I daresay, a good olive harvest." He raised his bowl to Elkanah and drained it in one gulp.

"We did well."

"We're all going to need to do better than well. Especially when the Sea People start raiding at will."

"That's the first I've heard of it. As far as I know, they have yet to move beyond the cities they've captured along the plain."

"They will, my boy, they will," he chuckled, as if he thought the prospect to be his idea of fun. Samuel and Lebiya exchanged glances as Nehum called Elkanah "boy," even though he was older by only a few years.

"My thought exactly," Izhar replied, raising his own bowl toward Nehum. Lebiya snorted like an ox to hear her brother currying Nehum, since she knew he'd be one of the first to criticize him behind his back. She also wondered if anyone else had noticed that Izhar was keeping up with Nehum's drinking, matching him bowl for bowl, drop for drop. Her brother was hard enough to live with when he was sober!

Samuel, however, heard none of the conversation. It was as if the boisterous conversation in the room began to grow more and more quiet until it seemed no more than the distant drone of a fly. All he could focus on were the boils.

Working at Eli's side had taught him many things, one of them being the variety of skin conditions that could afflict people. It had been the high priest's duty to examine skin eruptions and determine how they were healing in order to judge whether or not an individual was ritually pure enough to participate in worship.

Samuel had thus seen his share of skin problems, from simple pimples to discolorations heavy with pus and blackened blood. And now, as he stared down at his arm, he could see them starting to grow: tumors as large as a child's fist, swelling, receding, swelling, turning a sick shade of purple, threatening to burst, and then the sequence would repeat itself. Unable to move, he was convinced that if he uncovered his legs or his back or his stomach they too would show the same terrible dance. And the music that drove it was the same sad wail that had accompanied the marching of the mice through the field in his vision.

"Samuel!"

In an instant he snapped out of the trance. He saw an expression of concern on his father's face, skepticism on his half brothers', and Nehum looking as always extremely pleased with himself.

"Let's hear what you have to say, boy!" Nehum said, his bowl raised again. "Do you agree with me or with your brother here?"

"I'm sorry, sir—about what?"

Izhar rolled his eyes and exhaled. "About the Sea People!"

Something, perhaps the Spirit of prophecy itself, drew pieces of visions from different corners of Samuel's mind and pulled them together.

"He seems to think," Nehum said grandly as he indicated Shemed, "that with the ark in their possession they'll attack at any time, definitely before the early rains. I, on the other hand, have spoken with many of our neighbors and tribesmen and am convinced that they'll wait until after the early rains before mounting an assault."

"You're both mistaken," he said simply, his voice so soft that those seated toward the walls of the room had to strain to hear. "They will not attack. Not while the ark is in their possession."

"Lad, lad, you've been away for a while, so you've lost touch with the way things have become. We live in expectation of an attack, and with the Sea People holding the ark—"

"They won't keep it. The Sea People will return it to us one day. I don't know how or when, but they will."

A silence settled over the room, not so much because of what Samuel had said but because of the tone, the absolute certainty in his voice. For a second his brothers felt incensed, but their reaction turned to shock when Nehum spoke.

"Well, this changes everything, then, doesn't it? I mean, I've heard about this boy of yours, Elkanah. He's a seer, everyone says. And if he says the Sea People won't be attacking anytime soon, I think we can all celebrate and breathe a little easier." Breaking into a broad smile, he lifted his bowl one more time.

Nehum's statement stunned Elkanah and his sons, especially Samuel. Something had just happened, but he had no idea what. He looked at Lebiya, who only nodded as she refilled Nehum's drinking bowl.

The rest of the evening went by in a blur to Samuel. The only things he remembered distinctly were Nehum's almost constant requests for more wine and the dark looks his half brothers gave him after what he had said about the Sea People. The party finally broke up well after dark. That being the case, the host was expected to put everyone up for the night. Most simply slept where they were, after the girls had cleared away the plates and leftover food, a duty that had dropped on Lebiya's shoulders, as Elisheba had fallen asleep herself. Samuel pitched in to help, just wanting to put an end to things and looking forward to the morning, when everyone would leave.

"What happened with Nehum?" Samuel whispered to Lebiya as he extinguished all but one oil lamp in the room.

"What do you mean, what happened?"

"When I was telling him what . . . well, it had to be what the Lord showed me . . . I honestly didn't think he'd believe me."

"Why shouldn't he have believed you?"

Samuel started to answer, but before he could she held up her hand, then glanced toward the door leading out into the courtyard. They stepped out into the cold night air.

"Now," Lebiya said, still talking in a whisper, "why didn't you think he'd believe you?"

"Well, I disagreed with what he'd said before."

"But you also told him what he wanted to hear."

"I did?"

"I know Nehum. He called you a seer, and he's probably right, but it's not about prophecy, it's about his farmstead. Everything he says involves it in some way. You just assured him that he won't have to worry about losing his crops anytime soon. That's why he was so ready to believe you."

"And that's all?"

"Probably." She started to go back inside, paused, then turned back. "Did you mean it when you said that the Lord showed you the Sea People wouldn't be invading the highlands?"

"That's what it has to be. I've been too busy to think about it, but all of a sudden it came to me. It *had* to be the Lord—I couldn't have thought of it on my own."

"What happened to you, what you saw—was it anything like the first time?"

"No, I was asleep then, and at first I thought it was Eli calling me."

"And did God *say* that the Sea People wouldn't be attacking?"

"No, but it explains the visions of the mice and . . ."

"And what?"

"During the party I had another vision. I saw boils erupting all over my arms, and . . . and I also remembered the last time I saw Hophni and Phinehas carrying the ark of the covenant out of the tabernacle. I think God showed that to me as a way of indicating what the visions of the mice and the boils have in common. I believe that God is punishing the Sea People for keeping the ark. That's why I said they'll send it back someday."

Lebiya opened her mouth to say something, then closed it again. Finally she said, "I'll finish cleaning up inside," and then went in. Samuel glanced at the sky, saw that it was a cloudy night, and followed her.

★   ★   ★

It wasn't long before the early rains began. Their arrival along with a drop in temperature marked the change in the season. The rains softened the ground that the summer sun and winds had baked hard. At Shiloh Samuel had taken the cycle of seasons in stride. His main concern, after all, had been Eli's well-being and whether the rains would extinguish the fire burning in the bronze altar of sacrifice rather than whether the fields were ready for plowing and sowing. At night he would wrap himself in his blanket, listening to the raindrops drumming the roof of the tabernacle and gazing at the light of the menorah, knowing that he was safe.

Here at home, however, as the days went by it meant being shut up in the house along with everyone else. And there were a lot of people sharing what had seemed to Samuel when he first arrived to be a lot of space. But somehow, he learned, rainy days have a way of making indoor spaces grow smaller and smaller.

It didn't take much rain to soften the ground for plowing in order to plant the winter wheat and barley. The little wooden plows had only to scratch the surface of the soil, breaking the hard crust, to permit sowing. The sons of Peninah were eager to begin the task. It wasn't just a matter of wanting to get out of the house, which they were glad enough to do—it also had to do with being young men looking for ways to prove themselves as fullfledged adults.

The plow itself was simple. It consisted of a long pole lashed to the yoke worn by the two oxen the family kept for this purpose. The lower end of the pole held a stout stick that the person driving the oxen forced into the ground. The stick broke the soil and prepared it for planting.

Izhar had suggested that Samuel take a turn at plowing. He wasn't serious about it, of course. Beforehand, he told his brothers that he planned to tell Samuel that to accommodate the lay of the land he had to make sure he plowed all the furrows in the same direction. That meant instead of plowing the next furrow from the opposite direction, Samuel would have to bring the oxen back to where they'd started and then begin making the second furrow. It had seemed like a perfect jest until Shemed pointed out that what he'd mainly accomplish would be to tire out the oxen, something that their father wouldn't appreciate.

The sons of Peninah did the actual sowing of the seed. They made it quite clear that Samuel couldn't be expected to do as good a job as they did, even though it consisted of taking a handful of seed and casting it across the shallow furrows. Samuel received the task of walking behind the brothers with a tree branch. He would use the branch to sweep the seed into the furrows if it didn't land directly in them.

"And no dreaming on the job, seer!" Shemed taunted with a laugh.

Samuel did the best he could, and he received no visions as he worked. He was, in fact, somewhat disappointed by that fact. The work was back-breaking, and he would have welcomed a divine visitation just to break up the monotony.

The winter rains continued to come and go. Everyone felt miserable listening to them pound the roof of the house. Even worse, the water sometimes found its way indoors, dripping through the mud and clay surface. If it hadn't been raining they could have packed more mud onto the leaks and then rolled it flat to pack it in.

But until the storms slackened, there was nothing to be done about the situation. Except perhaps to pass the time by telling stories.

"Bet you wish you were back at Shiloh," Izhar said one day when everyone found themselves stuck indoors, trying to stay out of each other's way.

Samuel did not say anything.

"That's right," Shemed added, "eating beef and mutton every day, never having to lift a finger to grow so much as a blade of grass."

"Must've been nice," Manoah muttered.

"It wasn't like that," Samuel said testily.

"No, all you had to do was follow some old fool around all day."

"Eli wasn't a fool!" the boy shouted.

"Oh, look!" Izhar said. "The little dog knows how to stand on his hind legs!"

"That's enough!" Elkanah snapped.

"Well, I'm tired of him not knowing his place around here. And if he doesn't like it here, why doesn't he go back to Shiloh?"

"You want to know why I don't go back?" Samuel said with such vehemence that it frightened even Elkanah a little. "There's nothing left to go back to, that's why!

"Hundreds of people came to Shiloh to demand that Hophni and Phinehas get the ark so they could take it into battle against the Sea People. I never saw Eli so frightened as when everyone surrounded him, shouting for the ark. And Hophni . . . that look on his face . . . he knew exactly what was going on. He'd been preparing for just that moment. I'd listened to him putting that very notion into the heads of people for months."

Samuel clenched his hands into fists. "Eli looked devastated when they carried the ark off. Everyone else was cheering and shouting. But he knew what was happening, he knew what would come of this . . . and all he could do was cry."

Izhar and Shemed exchanged glances. They'd have made a jest at Eli's expense if they'd had their way, but now they didn't dare.

"The high priest went through the daily rituals, but I could see that his heart wasn't in it. And he'd glance toward the end of the valley where he'd last seen the ark, as if he expected to see Hophni and Phinehas bringing it back at any moment. Nobody tried to speak to him—I don't think he felt like talking anyway.

"Then came the day when I saw someone running up the valley toward us. When he got closer, I could see that he was covered with dirt and breathing hard. He almost fell down in front of Eli, and he said . . . he said . . . he said that the Sea People had won, they had taken the ark, and Hophni and Phinehas were dead.

"For a moment Eli just stared into the distance. His face . . . it was as if someone had struck him. Then he fell over backward and just lay there. I called to him and shook him, but . . . but he was dead."

As Samuel wiped a sleeve across his eyes nobody said anything.

"He just lay there and . . . I started crying. I don't know how long. Finally I looked up and around me. Everyone had panicked when they'd heard the news. It was horrible. People were running away, grabbing things, fighting over them. The sockets—the poles holding up the linen curtain around the sanctuary had silver sockets—people were digging them out with their bare hands . . . they were stealing anything they could find . . . it was as if everyone had gone insane with fear." Tears streamed down Samuel's face as he remembered.

"I didn't know what to do at first. Then I thought of Issachar. I found him at his tent. He didn't know what was happening—he was yelling at anybody he sensed near him, calling them names. I went up to him and . . . and told him about Eli. I started crying again. After a little he told me to explain again what happened to Eli. So I did. He said that we had to bury the high priest. I couldn't think where, so I asked him.

"We both dug his grave in the place where the tabernacle had stood. Some of the priests had stripped it, even taking the skins covering the tent. I saw the spot where the ark had stood in the Most Holy Place, and that's where we made Eli's grave. I don't know how long we worked, Issachar and I, but afterward he helped me drag the high priest's body to the grave.

"Then I took Issachar to the village of Shiloh and asked the potter there to help him find a place to go. Then I left and . . . I came here."

The rain was still falling outside as Samuel finished his story. For a long time nobody said anything. At last Lebiya broke the silence. "So everything's gone?"

Samuel slowly nodded.

"So what does that mean?"

"It means nothing has changed," Shemed sneered. "Everybody says that people are doing what they themselves think is right."

"Does that mean Samuel's a priest?" Lebiya asked.

"I think it means Father is the priest in this family now," the boy replied.

"So what does that make you?" Shemed asked, but Elkanah glared at him so he and his brothers kept their mouths shut.

"It makes Samuel what he's always been: a seer, someone with whom God has spoken," Hannah said.

Peninah's sons had long ago learned that Hannah was adamant on this point, however much they discounted the idea themselves. So they said nothing in response. But Samuel replied, "Shemed's right, Mother. What *does* that make me?"

"What do you mean?"

"At the sanctuary all we did was offer the sacrifices and perform the rituals. I knew what I was supposed to do because . . . because I grew up doing it. Eli even dressed me in the clothes of a high priest so I'd know what to do.

"But now there is no more high priest and no sanctuary. And . . . and I kind of miss it."

"What was there to miss?" Izhar demanded. "From what I heard, all you did there was sacrifice animals."

"It was more than that. We were doing what God had commanded everyone to do through Moses."

"Well, now there's no sanctuary and no Moses. As they say, everyone has to do what they think is right."

Samuel wanted to answer Izhar, but he couldn't think of anything to say. Besides, though he didn't want to admit it, Izhar was right. It was different at the sanctuary, where people from all of the tribes would seek Eli's counsel . . . when they weren't scolding him for the behavior of his sons. All this raced through Samuel's mind and would have discouraged him had he not felt something: 3-year-old Jedidah tugging at his elbow. The child looked up at him and inquired, "Who's Moses?"

"If you're looking for something to do, you can answer that question," Izhar chuckled. He had meant it derisively, for talking to a toddler was not his idea of doing something worthwhile.

"Why not?" Lebiya asked, shifting herself around to face Samuel.

It took only a moment for him to realize that even though he had no sacrifices or rituals to repeat, there was still value in passing on the knowledge of God's dealings with His people to someone who had yet to learn it. So as the child took a seat in front of him, and as the other family members with the exception of Peninah turned to listen, Samuel started to speak: "It began a long time ago, with the sons of our father Jacob . . ."

★   ★   ★

The rain had finished before the story, but nobody had noticed. Samuel had talked for more than an hour, telling of the enslavement of the children of Israel in Egypt, of the God who still watched over them in their misery, and of the unlikely child who grew up in the shadow of Pharaoh himself to lead them to eventual freedom.

Jedidah hung on every word, but still didn't hesitate to interrupt Samuel to ask, "What's a chariot?" or comment, "Moses was scared, huh?" Samuel had heard Hophni making speeches to the people, setting himself up not just as a priest but as a national leader. It felt good to Samuel to know that he wasn't just telling Jedidah what the child wanted to hear the way Hophni had done with the pilgrims to Shiloh.

And, it seemed, Jedidah wasn't the only one with questions. Twice Lebiya had breached etiquette by asking Samuel ones of her own. No one reprimanded her, probably because she had done it so often before that there was no point in anyone trying to do anything about it now. But Samuel noticed something else as well. Even as she tried to manage her children and such parts of the house that weren't under Peninah's control Hannah listened with a serenity and an understanding that he seldom saw in her. As for the rapt attention of the others, not daring to think that someone his age could be such a great storyteller, he reasoned that almost everyone in the family was simply unfamiliar with the ancient account. And if they didn't know *this* story, how many others were they ignorant about?

Samuel wrapped a cloak around Jedidah, who had dropped off to sleep at the part where Moses received the Ten Commandments on

Mount Sinai. Everyone else had separated for the evening. He then picked up the girl and brought her to the room where Hannah slept with her children. Finding a spot on the floor and wrapping Jedidah's own clothes tighter around her to keep out the chill, he looked up at the oil lamp burning on one shelf. It certainly wasn't the splendid golden menorah, but it made him smile to himself. Its light was a sign that, just as God hadn't abandoned His people during their time of slavery, so He hadn't rejected them now, even though the sanctuary had been destroyed and Eli was dead and everyone seemed to have their own ideas of how to follow God . . . if they followed Him at all.

The sanctuary was gone, he told himself. Though it still hurt to remember what had happened, he had to accept it. But that didn't mean his work had ceased. And if that now meant telling the ancient stories to the children of Hannah, he could accept that as well.

★   ★   ★

The rains continued for several days, so it was a while before the sons of Peninah could patch the roof. They gathered branches and wove them into a mat over the weak spot in the roof before patching it with mud and then rolling it flat.

Part of Samuel wished that he could have helped them, but they pointedly told him that it was men's work and that he should go back to being a wet nurse. He should have been angry at them, but decided it wasn't worth the bother. Also he knew that he shouldn't have laughed when, at the next heavy rain, the roof continued to leak, but he couldn't help it.

Besides, he was feeling more a part of the family as he worked at recalling not only the stories he had heard from Hannah before she had left him with Eli, but also the ones he had learned from the high priest himself. It seemed that he spent every evening that winter relating some story or other to his younger siblings, with the others inevitably listening in. Peninah and her sons may not have accorded Samuel any greater respect as a result, but neither did they absent themselves.

As for Lebiya, she listened as attentively as the younger children, and Samuel did not fail to notice. Finally he asked her about it one day as he watched her feeding twigs and straw into the dome-shaped clay oven in the courtyard to heat it for breadmaking. Elisheba, meanwhile, had finished kneading a fresh batch of dough and was forming it into balls for Peninah to flatten on a stone.

"No, I have never heard any stories like that," she said softly as she cast a furtive glance toward Peninah, who didn't seem to be paying close attention to her. "Mother never told us any of them, at any rate. I don't know whether she thought Father was supposed to do it or what."

"Didn't my mother tell any stories to her children?"

"Yes, but Peninah pretty much made sure we were all in another room when Hannah got started. I could only hear part of whatever she said."

"So why isn't my mother doing anything like that now?"

"I think Father has something to do with it. Now that you're back he doesn't want us to forget that you're his son as well. He really missed you when you were gone and always looked forward to seeing you when they went to Shiloh. I think he's especially proud of you."

"Really?"

"I guess seers don't know *everything,* do they?" she said with a grin as she snapped a little bundle of sticks in two and fed them into the oven. Even though the weather was still cold, she'd been sitting so close to the heated oven that she wiped the sweat from her brow. "I really wish I could have seen it. Shiloh, I mean."

"I wish it was still there to see."

They had to break off their conversation as Elisheba came over with a tray of bread dough. The process of baking was simple. Lebiya slapped the flat circles of dough against the heated inner surface of the oven and then removed them when they had finished baking. Lebiya glanced up into the sky. It was threatening to rain yet again, and she hoped that they could finish before the skies opened up.

"Blessings upon your house," a voice said behind them. Everyone turned to see a man dressed in well-worn clothing standing at the entrance of the courtyard. "Is the . . . is your father at home?"

"I'll get him," Samuel volunteered as he entered the house and emerged less than a minute later behind Elkanah.

"May I help you?" Elkanah inquired.

"Yes, well, it's just that . . . I mean . . ."

"Doesn't exactly have a way with words, does he?" Lebiya whispered to Samuel.

"We need . . . well, I need . . . and I was wondering if you could possibly . . . if it's not too much trouble . . ."

"What?" Elkanah finally asked.

"You're needed . . . I need . . . could you come to the village gate, please?"

Elkanah sighed. He had come to be respected, to a certain extent, by the people of Ramah. As a result, they occasionally asked him to take part in village discussions and decisions. As was customary, such councils met at the gate of the city, constituting an open court that held its deliberations in public.

"All right," Samuel's father said. "Let me get my cloak."

"And . . ."

Elkanah paused, wondering how long it would take the stranger to get to the point this time!

"And could you . . . could he . . . could you bring the seer?"

"The seer?"

"The seer!"

Lebiya smirked. "I think he means you," she said as she pushed Samuel forward. The request frankly shocked the boy, and he was glad that he hadn't fallen on his face when she had shoved him from behind.

"You are . . . you're the one . . . the seer?" the man questioned.

"I guess so." Samuel wondered if the visitor was going to change his mind.

"You'll come, please?"

Samuel looked back toward his father, who appeared just as thunderstruck as the boy himself by the summons. Still, Elkanah nodded before going into the house and emerging a short time later with two cloaks. The man was still stammering his thanks to both of them as they left.

★　★　★

"So what was it like?" Lebiya asked hours later as they ate dinner.

"It wasn't bad," Samuel replied when he and his father had returned home. The boy used a piece of bread to sop up the stew in the bowl in front if him. But he ate slowly because he was too excited to concentrate on the food.

"There were two other men at the gate when we got there," he said. "I'd never seen them before—they weren't at Jedidah's weaning party. One of the men scowled a lot and looked as if he were going to hit somebody. He reminded me a lot of Phinehas."

"Who?"

"One of the sons of Eli. Anyway, when we arrived the scowling man said Father was supposed to be the one in charge of the hearing. The man who came to get us—his name's Asher—said that the scowling man—his name's Joshua—had stolen something from him and wouldn't give it back. Only it took him a long time to say it because . . ."

"I think I can guess *why* it took so long," Lebiya interjected.

"Anyway, it turned out that the stolen object was Asher's cloak. Joshua said that he was entitled to it as a pledge and that Asher had no right to ask for it back."

"So what happened?"

"Well," Samuel hesitated, then turned to face Elkanah.

"No, go ahead, you're doing fine," his father nodded.

"Well, we sat down with men from the village on the stone benches lining the wall by the gate. There were other people there too, but mostly they stood around and listened. Then both Asher and Joshua told their sides of the story. At first it seemed as if Joshua was in the right. Asher *did* make the promise. But then I asked Asher how Joshua had gotten his cloak, and he said that Joshua had pretty much walked into Asher's house and pulled it off his shoulders."

"Is that such a bad thing?" Izhar asked.

"Of course it is! It states in the law of Moses that you're supposed to wait outside a man's house if you've come to get his cloak as a pledge."

"It does?" Lebiya said.

"I—I thought everybody knew that."

"Apparently not everybody does, certainly not Joshua," Elkanah commented.

"So did he give the cloak back?" Lebiya asked.

"I hope not," Izhar interrupted.

"Izhar!"

"I mean it, Father. What kind of an arrangement is it when someone promises you something in security and then won't give it up? That just isn't right!"

"It's not about that," Samuel spoke up. "There's nothing wrong with taking someone's cloak as a pledge, but you shouldn't seize a man's dignity along with it."

"And does it say *that* in the law of Moses, too?"

"Of course!"

The sons of Peninah exchanged glances. As much as they might have wanted to challenge Samuel on the point, they weren't familiar enough with the law to do so. In fact, they barely knew it at all, but weren't about to admit it.

"Anyway," Samuel went on, "Joshua finally admitted that Asher was right, so it was worked out that Joshua would keep Asher's cloak during the day, but he'd have to return it at night so Asher could have something to sleep in."

"Then what?" Lebiya continued.

"Then everyone there witnessed the agreement and that was it. Asher tried to give me something in payment, but I turned it down."

"What!"

For the first time in Samuel's presence Peninah finally said something. "He tried to pay you and you turned it down?"

"But he didn't have anything to give me—in fact, he didn't have much of anything. That's why he needed his cloak back."

"So what did he offer you?"

"I don't know—I stopped him before he could tell me."

"Elkanah," she shouted, "what kind of fool have you sired here? The first chance he has to add something to this household and he turns it down!"

"First off," Elkanah said, struggling to control his anger, "I approved of what Samuel did. A judge should be impartial, in nobody's debt, and showing nobody favor. Second, Asher made the offer only because he was too proud to admit that he didn't have anything to give but felt he had to go through the motions anyway.

Samuel couldn't have come away with anything more valuable than the sandals off of Asher's feet. Whatever the Lord had in mind when He gave Samuel the gift of prophecy, He certainly didn't intend anyone getting rich."

As Samuel listened he felt his stomach drawing into a tighter and tighter knot. Whatever elation he had experienced from his part in acting as a judge now vanished. The sons of Peninah, working at controlling their own rage, deliberately looked away. Lebiya glared at her mother with undisguised contempt. Hannah's other children huddled closer to her. Finally, Peninah stood and stormed out of the room. A second after she did, Samuel saw Elkanah run his fingers through his hair, pause a second, then follow her into the next room. Her sons departed a short time later as Hannah directed her children into their quarters, leaving Lebiya and Samuel alone.

"You had to see that sooner or later," the girl said at last, breaking the silence. "It isn't the first time they've fought over anything. But this was the first time you were in the middle of it."

"Do they . . . are they always like that?"

"No, not always, but some things always make one or the other of them angry, and I guess riches is one of them. Peninah believes that because her sons have put so much work into the place it's more her farm than Elkanah's."

"She really thinks that?"

"Maybe she only *feels* it, but I guess that doesn't make any difference."

"Does Father still—uh—love Peninah?"

"He won't divorce her, if that's what you mean. But I don't think he ever loved her as much as he loves Hannah. Still, this farm succeeds as well as it does because of the work of Mother's sons, and she won't let Father forget it. Ever."

Lebiya stood and extinguished all but one oil lamp. Before leaving the room, she turned to Samuel and said, "Sounds as if you judged an easy case today. I hope all your decisions are as simple."

All this time Samuel had been sitting with a piece of bread in his hand and what was left of his portion of stew in the bowl in front of him. Now he stared at it, then stood and walked out into the courtyard. There he scraped his bowl onto the pile of fodder for the goats they kept penned up there and added his crust of bread. Maybe *they'd* have an appetite for it.

★   ★   ★

Peninah's sons didn't need another reason to resent Samuel's presence, but now they had one. It took the form of people arriving every few days and asking to see Elkanah. The farmers and landowners, whether prosperous or destitute, requested his services in making a judgment at the gate. Elkanah would always take Samuel with him. The boy would always return enthusiastic, willing to talk at length about even the most mundane of disputes that they had settled there. Always he mentioned some point of the judgment in which something he had said, or some question he had asked, had been the deciding factor, speaking about it casually the way anybody else would talk about the weather. And always he arrived home with nothing to show for his work except the satisfied expression on his face.

Then, as the winter began losing strength and the time for the hoeing of the flax drew near, things began to change. The people still came, though not as frequently as before. It was, after all, a farming community, and with the rolling of the seasons everyone now had more work to do than in the dreary wintertime. But now the people didn't bother requesting Elkanah to accompany them. Instead they asked for Samuel or "the boy" or occasionally even "the seer."

The half brothers resented the demand on Samuel's time more than ever and even wondered out loud why Elkanah didn't share their feelings. Their father, though, had recognized the wisdom and compassion with which Samuel made his deliberations and didn't hesitate to summon him. After a time, the sons of Peninah began avoiding the boy when he returned from the gate, and since Hannah's children were too young to be interested, that left Lebiya as his sole audience when he reported what had taken place. But she made up for it in sheer interest.

"Did you do anything like this before—back at Shiloh?"

"Not until the very end. Most people asked Eli to decide things for them. After all, he was the high priest."

"Is that where you learned how to do it?"

"No. I learned other things, though, and I guess they helped."

"What other things?"

"Mainly the things I'd see happening in the sanctuary every day. I would notice this one farmer, for instance, presenting a sin offering at the tabernacle. The man didn't come every day, but he might as well have. He always made the same offering, and he was always angry at someone or something when he did it. Actually, I think he was angry at himself.

"Anyway, I thought about it and eventually found myself wondering why he kept committing the same sin again and again if he resented giving the offerings. It's as if it never occurred to him to stop breaking the law."

"Maybe he couldn't stop."

"Or maybe he didn't try."

"I don't think you can know either way."

"I know, and that's what makes it so hard, except . . ."

"Except that God talks to you."

"Sometimes. Usually not at the gate, but He still does."

"What about?"

"So far, the same things I've already told you about: the mice and the boils. I've seen the same images three times now."

"You haven't mentioned it," Lebiya said, surprised and a little hurt.

"I didn't want to say anything around the others."

She thought a moment. "I can see what you mean. All they'd probably do is complain that you haven't had a different vision. 'If you see something new, then we'll believe you,'" she said, managing a fair impression of Izhar. "Forget about them. They wouldn't believe you if an ox fell on them from the sky."

Samuel couldn't help smiling. "Thanks."

"For what? I've just been listening."

"But that's enough."

★   ★   ★

Spring was coming at last, and not a moment too soon. The house seemed to close in on its occupants as the rains tapered off. The immediate goal was to deal with the crop of flax.

While wool was the primary clothing material, people grew flax to make linen. Yet Samuel recognized from the linen garments he saw in the village that the local plants didn't produce the type of fine fabric that Eli and the priests had worn. The fibers were coarser and darker, more closely resembling those in his own linen garments. He never resented the difference—they were priests, after all. As Levites they were entitled to wear the better garments as they went about their tasks.

Still, Samuel had never become acquainted with the processes by which the farmers turned flax into linen. And he wasn't looking forward to learning from the sons of Peninah, either.

It began the day when Shemed walked into the house, a stone-bladed hoe resting on his shoulder. Since his brothers obviously recognized what it meant, Samuel pretended to know as well. And since nobody barred him from following them, he accompanied them outside.

Peninah's sons even at best seemed to have a mixed opinion of Samuel capabilities. They didn't consider him big enough or strong enough to wield a hoe to loosen the roots of the flax stalks, but they thought he could pull up the stalks by the roots and lay them out on the ground. To make linen the stalks had to be uprooted when the bases were yellowish and the seeds were not yet ripe. Young plants provided the best fiber for linen, while older stalks would yield coarser fibers used to make rope.

Samuel couldn't help noticing that after they had finished hoeing, they went off to the edge of the field and sat around talking and laughing while leaving him to pull up all the plants. The one time he tried to join them, Shemed picked up a small rock and tossed it at him. It wasn't all that large and the aim was terrible, but Samuel got the message. He went back to uprooting flax.

Although Samuel tried to convince himself that what he was doing was important, that it was helping the family, his half brothers continued to let him do all the stooping and pulling and carrying. He could only stop for a few seconds before his brothers started pelting him, not with stones but with insults. "Not like the sanctuary, is it?" "If those old men by the gate saw the way you work, maybe they'd think twice about asking for your opinion." "What you're doing now is *real* work—get used to it!"

But Samuel *didn't* want to get used to it. As far back as he could remember, even before Hannah had taken him to Shiloh she had told him, with great love and solemnity, that the Lord had appointed a special work for him and that he should always remember that. But with his back aching and his knees hurting and the sweat running down and stinging his eyes, he wondered if, with the sanctuary destroyed, this wasn't what he was meant for after all. He forgot all about the times he'd helped with the deliberations at the gate and the praise he had received. Perhaps pulling up flax stalks was all he'd ever be good for.

The sons of Peninah didn't stir until Samuel had collected the last of the flax. Then they started bundling the stalks for the retting process. They ended up making only four bundles that they carried themselves. For a moment it occurred to Samuel that they might be rewarding him for doing most of the work up to this point. That made him feel a little better as they approached the house. Later he would discover that they would dry those four bundles for rope fibers. The rest would become raw material for linen.

As the four half brothers spread their stalks in the courtyard, Samuel passed Elkanah as he was walking out of the house. Pausing for a moment, he listened to the brothers talk to Elkanah.

Immediately his heart sank. He couldn't catch all of what they said, but what he heard was enough. "Don't know why we expected anything of him . . . absolutely useless out there . . . doesn't know anything . . . we tried being patient . . ."

Having heard enough, Samuel raced out of the courtyard and around to the side of the house. A narrow staircase led up to the roof. Half blinded by his anger, he stumbled his way up it.

"Watch it!" someone called out to him when he reached the roof. He saw clothing laid flat everywhere. Standing in the middle of the garments, Lebiya was busy flattening a woolen cloak heavy with moisture. "Watch where you step! I don't need to wash these all over again."

Feeling suddenly exhausted, he sat down heavily on the low parapet that edged the roof. Stepping lightly between the articles of clothing, Lebiya walked toward him, then deftly seated herself in a small open spot in front of him. "I heard what they were saying about you. I hope you didn't believe them."

Samuel didn't reply as he ran the back of his hand across his eyes.

"I also know what liars they can be. I saw what happened in the flax field."

"How?" he asked.

Lebiya smiled wryly. "For a seer, you have a hard time noticing what's right in front of you. Look over there," she said as she nodded toward the field.

Samuel did. "So?"

"So now try standing up."

Then he finally understood what she meant. From the rooftop he could clearly see the spot where the flax had been growing.

"And I saw how they were treating you out there, making you do all the work after they had loosened the roots."

His face flushed, Samuel lowered his head.

"If it'll make you feel any better," she went on in a softer voice, "I don't think Father really believes them. You might want to talk to him about it later on, when the fools aren't around."

"I will, thanks," he said, adding, "Why are you telling me this?"

Lebiya got to her feet, slapping the dirt from her clothes. "It's not important."

"No, I really want to know."

She paused, then sat down next to him on the wall.

"You haven't been here that long, so you don't know what it's really like. But for as far back as I can remember, there have been a lot of bad feelings in this house. Nobody says anything, but everybody is at war with everybody else. When I was little, only as old as Jedidah, I started saying whatever filled my heart, and I usually got punished for it because somebody didn't like it. Peninah, mostly." She studied him a moment. "I don't know how you feel about my talking about my mother like that, but there it is.

"For a while, when I was older, I barely said two words a day for fear of starting an argument or offending somebody. That wasn't very helpful either. I still had the same feelings, but it was as if . . . as if I was just keeping them in my belly and letting them make me sick. Do you understand what I'm saying?"

"I think so."

"That's more than Peninah and the fools have ever done. It got so bad that when I began to . . . to . . ." She paused, and her face turned as red as a sunset.

"Started having your monthly impurity?"

"Is that what you called it at Shiloh?"

"That's how Eli referred to it."

"Well, I was feeling so many things—anger, sadness, fear, and all at the same time—that I thought I was going to burst. It was strange," she said with a half smile, "but it wasn't until then that I got the idea of talking to Hannah.

"I wish I'd thought of it earlier. You have a very wise mother, and as compassionate as she is smart. I used to think that was a bad combination, mostly because Peninah said it was. I don't think that way anymore.

"She helped me through that time, helped me to see what was happening and what was going to happen. That's when I started to trust her.

"We talk whenever we can, but not in front of Peninah. She's convinced that Hannah is nowhere near as capable of running the house as she is, and she *is* right about that. Still, I'd give anything to be able to say Hannah is my mother instead of Peninah."

"I . . . never knew."

"You've got company. I don't think the fools realize it, either, and I want to keep it that way."

"I won't say anything to them."

"I didn't ask, but thank you." She glanced up at the sun. It was midday already. She then picked up an empty wicker basket that she had used to carry the laundry up to the roof. "Come on, let's get inside before they know we're *both* crazy!"

Samuel stood. "But what am I going to do about them?"

"There's not much you *can* do," she said as she started down the stairs. "You know what you did and didn't do, no matter what they say. Believe the truth."

"It's not always easy."

"I know, but think about this: maybe there's a reason people from Ramah have been asking for *you* to serve as a judge instead of one of *them."* Then with a sly smile, she left him.

*   *   *

In order to actually use the flax in weaving, it had to go through several processes. First, the stems were soaked in the retting tanks—basins of stagnant water. Timing was critical. The flax had to soak long enough for the fibers of the stalk to separate from the core, but not so long that they would discolor. After a little more than a week, the stalks were spread out to dry, usually on the rooftops, as in the story of Rahab and the Israelite spies. One had to be careful not to mix the roots with the tops to avoid problems extracting the fibers. Finally, the family would separate the fibers from the thin outer layer and woody core by gently beating or rolling the stalks. The brothers began this task one day after the midday rest.

With the stalks laid out flat on the ground, two of them took shepherd's rods and the other two simple grain flails, two pieces of wood joined by a length of rope running between two of the ends. With them they would beat the flax stalks. Later the family would comb out the fibers for spinning. They would try to keep the fibers as long as possible for the best thread. The broken fibers would go into coarser linen or lamp wicks.

The brothers didn't invite Samuel to join them in the beating process, which suited him fine. Something about the way they glanced in his direction before slamming their flails against the flax stalks told him that they were thinking, *Too bad this isn't you!*

As he slipped out of the doorway and back into the house he remembered what Lebiya had said to him about him knowing what he had done or not done when he had uprooted the flax stalks. But he still struggled with a number of questions, all of them about what he was supposed to do to serve the Lord.

At first he thought that it was a matter of growing up. *Maybe,* he told himself, *I'll have a better idea of how to serve Him when I get older.* But then he remembered that it hadn't been that long ago that the Lord had revealed to him the fall of the house of Eli. And he still received visions. In fact, he'd had three separate ones about the mice and of the boils now, though he hadn't told anyone except Lebiya. Whatever the Lord meant for him to do, he told himself with some hesitation, He seemed to want Samuel to be doing it now.

Then he considered whether it might be a case not of "what" and "when" but of "where." Perhaps he had to go somewhere else, as when Hannah had taken him to Shiloh when he was 4. Once there, he'd learn what God had in mind for him. But he gave up on this idea as well. If his mother had any other ideas about taking him somewhere, she hadn't shared them with him. Nor had the Lord told him anything, and He was certainly in a better condition to direct his life than Hannah. No, he finally realized, in spite of the fact that the house was overcrowded and bad feelings abounded—in spite of Peninah's imperiousness and her sons' hostility—this was where he was meant to be for the moment. And it was where he was supposed to serve the Lord.

But always in back of all those questions lurked the biggest one: "How should I serve God?"

Samuel remembered when Eli would sit at the entrance to the sanctuary courtyard, settling disputes and citing points of the law of Moses. Even more than what he had heard from Hannah as a toddler before coming to Shiloh, Samuel's formal education in the law and its intricacies had happened almost accidentally as he stood next to Eli and listened to him. He had no way of knowing how much of the law he had actually learned during those years—there was no real way to test one's knowledge—but he felt that he now understood quite a bit.

Still, what had he done with it? The disputes people asked him to help settle weren't all that important. One person borrowed from a neighbor and either couldn't or wouldn't pay him or her back. Another alleged that someone had moved a property marker, while his opponent laid the same charge against him. Two individuals agreed that there should be restitution because a stray animal had ruined a crop, but they disagreed on the amount.

Such disputes hardly seemed all that important to Samuel. They reminded him more of fights between Jedidah and Elisheba, and he was in the role of Hannah stepping in between them and settling the matter. Something seemed very upside down about adults, the age of his parents and even older, having their problems settled by a boy.

Then Samuel noticed a curious thing about those sessions in

which he had participated. At each one the same old man came to listen and to watch the disputes, as if he had no other business to attend to. And always, when one of the people in the discussion would say something that would get the tongues of the onlookers wagging, he'd always shake his gray head and always mutter the exact same words: "It's a sign of the times, it is."

Perhaps I'm one of those signs as well, Samuel thought. Maybe grown-ups acting like children and having to be told by a child how to behave was also a sign of the times.

He didn't ponder this for long because he suddenly noticed from inside the house that the brothers had stopped their work. Someone was walking into the courtyard. Samuel couldn't make out what the visitor was discussing with them, but from the way Shemed glanced at the house with a dark and resentful expression Samuel knew the man was asking for him.

When Samuel stepped outside, the stranger seemed surprised. "I was told to ask for Samuel," he said with a slight hesitancy in his voice. "Are you he?"

"Yes."

"Well, I was expecting someone . . . never mind. I was told you settle disputes."

"If the price is right," Shemed said in the kind of whisper meant to be heard.

"Never mind him," Samuel said as he saw the man reach for a small bag hanging from his belt. "What do you want?"

"If you could be at the gate tomorrow morning, please. I can explain it then."

"All right. At sunrise?"

The stranger nodded.

"Tomorrow at sunrise, then."

"Thank you very much," the man said to Samuel, then left the courtyard.

"Getting an early start, aren't you?" Shemed remarked in a way that made Samuel think of a dog growling.

"That's when he wants me to be there," Samuel said as he shrugged.

"Then he can furnish your breakfast, because I don't think

Mother will be getting up to do it herself, will she?"

Grinning cruelly, the other brothers nodded in agreement, then went back to beating the flax stalks.

"Samuel?"

Startled, he turned around in time to see Hannah emerge from her room with Ahitub in her arms. "Who was that?"

"Someone who wants me to be at the gate tomorrow morning at sunrise."

"That's rather early, isn't it?"

"That's when he said to be there."

"Well, let me know when you'll be leaving, so I can have some food ready for you."

"All right. Thanks."

"Is something the matter?"

"No," he said.

Hannah stared at him with an expression that asked, "Are you certain?"

Before he could answer, though, Jedidah came out of Hannah's room. As soon as she saw Samuel she broke into a broad grin. "Tell me a story!" she demanded, for in her mind Samuel had become synonymous with storytelling.

"All right," he said, smiling, as he seated himself on the floor, and while he tried to think of what story to tell the brothers continued to beat the flax stalks until it sounded like hailstones pummeling the courtyard.

Samuel knew that during supper that evening the brothers would make his behavior sound worse than it was, and they didn't disappoint him.

"Admit it, Father," Shemed insisted, "he doesn't know how to do a man's job, and I wonder if he ever will."

"He's not being asked to do man's work," Elkanah said wearily, tired of hearing the continual complaints from his other sons.

"You're right, you know," Izhar added. "So far all he's shown himself good for is women's work."

"That's not true!" Samuel blurted.

"Well, what would you call gossiping at the city gate all day and telling stories to babies?"

"I'm *not* a baby!" Jedidah protested.

"He seemed to be doing all right for himself earlier today," Lebiya said in a steady voice.

"What's *that* supposed to mean?" Shemed demanded.

"Look who's coming to his defense!" Izhar said.

"Shemed! Lebiya! That's enough from both of you. And you too, Izhar."

"If you know so much," Lebiya said as she cast a sullen glare at Shemed, "what work would you have him do?"

"It doesn't matter, so long as he does it somewhere else."

"Why did he have to come back here anyway?" Izhar complained.

"I *had* to come back here!" Samuel protested. "This is my home! The sanctuary was destroyed."

"Too bad you didn't get wiped out with it."

Lebiya had hoped that Elkanah would stick up for Samuel for once instead of letting the four fools have free rein. But the family exchanged the usual round of accusations and insults before everyone went to their respective quarters. Hannah remained behind to clean up from the meal and to deal with the youngest children. Lebiya had given her parents a "Do we have to go through this at every meal?" glare before turning her back on them. And Samuel, the immediate cause of the conflict, had sat left alone as the storm whirled around him.

Samuel looked at Hannah, who stared back. Neither said anything. The situation had deteriorated past the point of words. Instead he simply helped her tidy up.

★   ★   ★

Samuel had gotten used to rising early at Shiloh to help Eli prepare for the morning sacrifice. As a result, he wasn't all that hungry when he told Hannah that he was leaving to go to the gate at Ramah.

With quiet efficiency Hannah pulled together a breakfast for Samuel: a loaf of bread and the last of some cheese. She put them in a sack so Samuel could eat on the way.

The morning air was chilly, but in an invigorating way and not threatening like the cold that reaches inside and takes hold of one's bones to announce that winter would soon be here. As he walked toward Ramah, Samuel found that he had more of an appetite than he thought. His thirst also increased as the sun rose and the day became warmer. As a result, his rations were long gone by the time he reached the village gate.

The same men were gathered there as always: the old, the self-important, the idle, or the merely curious. Samuel recognized the man who had spoken to him yesterday and walked over to him.

"My brother, with whom I share a piece of property, said he would be here early so we could settle this matter. Looks as if he's late. I'm not surprised. He probably knows he's in the wrong. The problem is that he . . ."

But Samuel had stopped listening, for something had caught his attention, something that sent a wave of memories rolling through him.

The gate was the closest thing the village had to a public forum. As such, people gathered there for all sorts of reasons and not just to adjudicate lawsuits. Traveling peddlers would set out their wares, calling out to those who passed by in the hope that they would look and, having done so, would decide that they needed what was being sold. Scribes—those who knew how to read and write—waited to draft whatever documents people needed, from bills of sale to correspondence. And others sought work.

Samuel had seen two men about 60 cubits from where he stood. They were talking to virtually every man who passed them by, asking, begging, pleading for work. It wasn't an unusual sight at the gate. But there was something about these men, something familiar . . .

With a start, Samuel realized what it was. He *knew* them! Levites, they had been priests at the sanctuary . . . when there had *been* a sanctuary.

It had never occurred to Samuel to wonder what had happened to those who had abandoned it upon Eli's death. Everyone, it seemed, had simply scattered and vanished. But now here were two of the priests, still wearing their linen garments. But their robes were fraying and dirty, and the look on their faces was haunted and fearful. The tribe of Levi had received no land when Joshua had divided Canaan. It was expected that the entire tribe would be supported by the offerings of the sanctuary.

But now it no longer existed, and their once-easy lifestyle had vanished with it. How had they survived the winter, Samuel wondered, when the most that any farm family could do was to wait for the rains to let up? Had they been begging all this time? Some of the priests had lived with their families at Shiloh—what had become of the wives and children? Samuel had been able to return home to his parents. Did these two even *have* a home?

". . . which is what I've been telling him all along! Now, I ask you . . ."

"I'm sorry," Samuel said, as if waking from a troubled sleep. "I think we should wait for your brother to arrive."

"Well, if he doesn't, don't say I didn't warn you. You'll have come all this way for nothing."

"It's a sign of the times, it is!" Samuel heard an old man proclaiming from the edge of the crowd that had gathered.

When midday came and the other party in the case had not arrived, the first man asked Samuel for his judgment. Samuel decided that he had been in the right, but he added that everyone should reconvene at the gate when the brother finally did show up. Everyone regarded his suggestion as the height of wisdom and roundly complimented him for it. Under Samuel's direction and with noticeable reluctance, the first brother took an oath that he would notify him should the other arrive. Samuel received an offer to rest during the midday in the home of the first man but declined, accepting instead an invitation to go to the home of someone unconnected with the case.

The host, a man named Keilah, immediately started chattering in a friendly way with Samuel. The individual had a haggard, haunted look about him, though, as he started to lead Samuel toward his home. Suddenly Samuel stopped.

"You were at Shiloh, weren't you?"

Keilah paused, turning toward him with head low.

"So you remember. Yes, I left . . . I don't know how many years ago. It was about a year after your friend Abdon departed."

"I remember. I was 8 when he went away."

They said no more until they arrived at Keilah's one-room house. Inside he introduced Samuel to his wife. The young woman was pale with a thin face and seemed to be in a losing battle to control a small naked boy who must have been between 2 and 3 years old and who eluded her with the agility of a gazelle.

"Taphath," Keilah said to his wife, "you remember Samuel here? He was at Shiloh."

"I remember," she said as she caught hold of the wriggling toddler. "I always saw you with Eli."

"We'll . . . say no more about that," Keilah added. "I've asked Samuel to rest with us until after midday." He turned to Samuel. "We couldn't expect you to go home until later."

"I'll get you some water," the woman said, losing her grip on the boy as she went into a corner to pour water into a cup for Samuel. Normally Samuel would have declined it—he thought that his being a judge demanded that he not be in anyone's debt or favor. But he understood that the gift of water was part of the code of hospitality by which his people lived, and from the few possessions he could see in the room the couple had nothing more substantial that they could have offered him anyway.

"Forgive my son," Keilah said as he scooped the laughing child into his arms. "He won't keep anything on."

"I know, I have a sister who's about that age." Samuel recognized, however, that Jedidah wasn't allowed to go about without clothes—Hannah saw to that. It occurred to him that the reason for the child's nakedness might be because his parents couldn't afford to clothe him.

"I saw two other men today," Samuel said to Keilah after receiving the cup of water and taking a sip. "Weren't they at Shiloh too?"

"Which ones? Doesn't matter," he said with a sigh and a dismissive wave of his hand. "There are a lot of us abroad now. I've talked with some of them. They scattered when Eli died because they thought the Sea People were attacking."

"They never did."

"I know that now."

"What have you been doing?"

"When I came here I started by helping my wife's father. He had been a tanner but had gotten so old that he was ruining more hides than he cured. When he died last year, I took over his trade. It's not much, but it keeps us fed."

And that's about all, Samuel thought to himself. "Why did you leave?" he then asked.

"Probably for the same reason Abdon did. I knew he couldn't get along with Hophni and Phinehas and the way they acted. Neither could I. I had to get out."

All through their conversation Samuel felt extremely uncomfortable. It was obvious Keilah had fallen on hard times, but it would have been pointless to blame him for it, to say that it was because he had abandoned his Levitical calling. Now everyone who had served at the sanctuary was in the same situation. It only brought home to Samuel with greater force the fact that despite having to deal with the sons of Peninah, he was still in a far better position than some.

As the temperature rose, everyone by a kind of wordless mutual agreement took their midday rest. The gathering heat, though still mild by summer standards, seemed to be the only thing that slowed Keilah's son down as he snuggled next to his mother. Samuel received a spot on the floor close to the doorway, just about the only place where any air flowed into the room aside from a mere slit of a window set high on the same wall.

But Samuel didn't drift off to sleep right away. He had been living with the memory of the fall of the sanctuary of Shiloh for the past months. The death of Eli had pushed the fate of just about everybody else connected with the place from his mind. But there was no escaping it now that he had seen what had become of Keilah. Multiply that by the dozens of priests and novices who had served there, and add in their families, and the sheer misery of it weighed on Samuel's heart like a stone.

He said nothing about his thoughts as Keilah escorted him to the gate several hours later, but he did ask a question: "What's going to happen to the priests?"

"I don't know," the man replied, running his fingers through his hair. "The main hope is to make it through to the harvest in two months. It'll be easier to find work then than it is now. If there's no work here, we can always try some place such as Beth-Shemesh."

Samuel told him the location of his family's farm. "I don't know what our harvest will be like, but you can glean there if you want to." He couldn't promise any more, because he didn't know whether Elkanah and his sons would welcome the idea of hiring anyone to help with the crop. But he promised himself that he would send word to Keilah if he could convince his family. With a final exchange of thanks, the two parted company, and Samuel began the trek home.

★   ★   ★

The next day he asked Lebiya, "Does Father hire workers to help with the harvest?"

"Sometimes. More often than not, we do the work ourselves, no matter how long it takes. Mother seems to think that hiring people is just asking for trouble. Why?" she asked, a trace of suspicion in her voice.

"I saw some men in town yesterday. They used to be priests at Shiloh and were looking for work."

"You didn't promise them anything, did you?"

"No, but I thought—"

"Take my advice," she said, lowering her voice. "Say nothing to Mother about it. She has no use for hiring people—says it's just another way to have someone take food out of our mouths. It's bad enough that she and our father get into a fight every year about her sending the fools out to chase off the gleaners."

"Does Father agree with her about not hiring laborers?"

"He didn't used to. But now that you're back home he's got one less reason to pay for extra help. Believe me, they're going to run you ragged when harvesttime comes."

His mind repeatedly kept going back to the priests he had seen at the gate at Ramah. Samuel resolved, then and there, to try to learn as much about farming as possible. Maybe the Lord meant him to be a seer, but it couldn't hurt to know other things.

★   ★   ★

Agricultural skills didn't come easy for him, however. No matter how hard he tried to learn, the work itself was harder, a realization brought home with force when Elkanah took him along with his other sons to tend their flocks during lambing season.

Samuel had mixed feelings about the expedition. He had seen more lambs in his time at Shiloh than most shepherds ever would. The priests offered two lambs per day for the sins of the nation. While other priests did most of the work of dismembering the animal and offering it on the large altar of sacrifice in the courtyard, it was Eli who twice daily cut the throat of the animal and who mingled its blood with incense and fire and prayer in the holy place. The boy had lost the ability to feel sorry for the lambs long ago.

Yet he was also largely ignorant as to how people took care of the sheep. Eli had told him that he needed the boy at the tabernacle and that shepherding wasn't really any of his concern. Samuel had accepted it without question. Yet now, as he and his father and half brothers approached the low stone enclosure out in the pastureland where the sheep had been driven earlier, he became overly conscious of his ignorance.

"You ever take part in a lambing while you were at Shiloh?" Elkanah asked as he leaned on the wall, surveying the small flock that the family owned.

"No," Samuel admitted. Two of the brothers snickered.

"That'll be enough, you two," Elkanah cautioned. "It can get pretty bloody," he added, turning back to Samuel.

"Blood doesn't bother me."

"Oh, really?" The statement seemed to challenge Shemed.

"Really! Bulls, sheep, lambs, oxen—I've watched them all being sacrificed."

Shemed let the matter drop. For Samuel, however, the brief exchange was nothing short of invigorating. For once he'd been able to stand up to the half brother without apology, without pleading ignorance. *Too bad it doesn't happen more often,* he told himself.

Samuel didn't have much time to savor this triumph, however, as the others got to work almost immediately. They had come into the field to stay for the duration and wouldn't leave until the lambing concluded.

While Elkanah directed Samuel to help Zaccur and Manoah set up a temporary shelter for everyone, their father and the other two sons began wandering through the sheep, looking for the pregnant ewes.

Samuel had been with the flocks at Shiloh a handful of times, but he never remembered them being so noisy. Every sheep in the pen bleated enough for five. What made matters worse was that he had a hard time telling which sheep were pregnant and which weren't. His experience had been limited strictly to lambs and the problem had never come up before. Once more he realized just how wide the gulf was between his experience at Shiloh and life on his father's farm. When Manoah yelled for him to stop dreaming and help unload the donkey that had carried their supplies, Samuel was grateful.

After helping to pitch the small tent at the edge of the pen, Samuel noticed that people from other farmsteads were doing the same at their own enclosures. Soon Elkanah called his sons over to a large ewe that was bleating piteously.

"Samuel, roll up your sleeves. I need your help."

The boy might have felt proud if it weren't for the sight that greeted him. The ewe was already in labor, and even though Samuel had never attended a birthing before, he still sensed that it would have been difficult to make sense of what he was seeing. Already visible were a lamb's nose and two . . . no, three . . . hooves, but there was something wrong. The small hooves stuck out at crazy angles.

"She's carrying twins," Elkanah hastened to explain. "You need to find out which legs belong to which lamb so we can deliver them one at a time."

His face pale, Samuel looked at his father. "Why me?"

"Your hands are the smallest. I know you can do it," he hastened to add.

Swallowing hard, the boy eased his hand inside the ewe. He tried to follow one of the hooves but almost immediately felt it jerk away from his touch. Finding it a second later, he realized that it was a hind hoof of the other lamb. As he pulled his arm out he suppressed a powerful urge to be sick, then slid his hand along another leg, this time belonging to the lamb with the protruding muzzle. Aided by Elkanah, he managed to help deliver first one lamb, then the other.

It was a new sight for Samuel to see the lambs draw breath, to shake their heads to accustom themselves to this new world, to start their high-pitched bleating, and to seek their mother's milk through that instinct built into them by their Creator. It was also new to find himself with his arms up to his elbows inside a live animal. He had witnessed the slaughter of so many animals that he had become numb to it. But now, since it was something that he'd never done before, it overwhelmed him more than the sight of flayed carcasses. Again he swallowed the urge to be sick and did as Elkanah instructed.

Finally Samuel sat back on the ground when it was all over, breathing hard and with his arms covered in fluid. He wanted to hear Elkanah's reaction to what he had just done, what he had just gone through. Had he done a good job? The lambs were alive—that counted for something. But as he turned toward his father, Shemed was calling Elkanah over to another ewe, and Izhar was pulling him to his feet by the collar of his robe.

"Get used to it," Izhar said.

The next two days were a blur. When the ewes were not in labor the men spent the time waiting and watching out in the open, for Samuel learned that even in pastureland divided off by low stone walls, there was danger of someone taking advantage of the confusion by helping themselves to a sheep or two from someone else's flock. That must have been why Samuel sensed something when he saw Elkanah or his brothers conversing with a neighbor—he felt a slight wariness, a sense of mistrust. As engrossed as everybody seemed to be in the chaos of lambing, they were not too busy to keep watch over their own. Despite Samuel's almost total exhaustion he couldn't help remembering the covenant between Jacob and Laban—their way of saying, "May the Lord keep His eye on you even when I can't."

And the watching went on day and night. Because a sheep could be stolen or a ewe could go into labor at any time, somebody had to remain awake at all times. Elkanah tried to divide the duty evenly among his sons, but as often as not one of the sons of Peninah assigned to keep watch with Samuel simply told the boy that he was going to sleep, that he'd better not wake him or Elkanah unless a ewe started lambing, and that he was on his own.

Finally, after two of the longest days and nights Samuel had ever spent, he and the others returned home in the evening. Samuel felt torn between sheer exhaustion and the need to sleep as soon as he had lain down, and the hunger that came from eating too little in haste out in the open. It seemed at first that hunger would win out, for he simply stood in the doorway to the house—though it would be more accurate to say he held himself up by leaning on it—watching the preparation of the evening meal. They had brought one of the sheep with them for this purpose, and Samuel stared as the family quickly slaughtered it.

The boy was so tired that it took him a while to realize just what he was seeing. Finally he recognized that they were cooking the lamb in a way that he wasn't used to. "You can't do that!" he said out loud as a half dozen heads turned to look at him.

Peninah, who was supervising the preparation of the meal, didn't seem to hear what he had said.

"Get it out of there!" he said as he staggered more than walked toward the pot. Shemed caught him by the arm before he'd gone two steps.

"What are you babbling about now?"

"The tail . . . the tail of the sheep . . . it's almost all fat!"

"Yes, and that's what makes it the best part. What's your point?"

"We're not supposed to . . . to eat the fat . . . the fat . . . from a . . . sacrifice," Samuel said, his voice fading away.

"I give up!" Shemed declared as he flung Samuel away from him and the boy fell to the ground. "He's been here half a year and he still thinks he's at Shiloh! Well, I've lost my patience with him! He'll never amount to anything around here." The other sons of Peninah murmured their agreement.

"And if you don't want anything to eat because it's not good enough for you and your priests' ways," Izhar added, "I'll eat it myself."

"You'll have to fight me for it first!" Manoah added.

Picking himself off the ground, his appetite gone, Samuel staggered into the house and collapsed onto his usual spot. He hoped against hope that sleep would overtake him.

It didn't. The only thought that filled his mind was that in all his time at home he had failed. He had not only not succeeded in becoming a farmer, he had failed in a more fundamental way: he had not lived as he had at Shiloh. What was rigorous but still possible when he dwelled among the priests and novices at Shiloh was well-nigh impossible now. People at Shiloh had looked on him with curiosity and even occasional hatred, and he had learned to cope with it. What he hadn't expected when he returned home was this crushing lack of respect from his half brothers. Samuel had received honor at Shiloh, first when he assisted the high priest, then in his own right as someone considered to possess the holy spirit of prophecy. Then he had felt it again when people asked him to settle law cases at the city gate.

But here, in what was supposed to be home, under the very gaze of Elkanah and Hannah, the rest of the family regarded him as some kind of servant. Lower, in fact. No matter how hard he tried to fit in with farm life, he simply could not. And maybe Shemed was right. Perhaps he never would.

Alone in the room, the sounds of self-congratulation drifting in along with the scent of the stew, Samuel allowed himself the luxury of weeping.

It was later that evening that Hannah had found him sitting outside the house, staring up at the sky, seemingly oblivious to the weather. He told her of his growing sense that he was a failure. And he only hinted at what he would have preferred more than anything—to return to Shiloh.

Only Shiloh no longer existed.

Finally Samuel had to admit to himself that even though his mother and father lived in this place, even though they still cared for him, the farmstead was not his home. It could never be his home. Even if Peninah and her sons were to disappear, swallowed up by the earth as Korah's rebels had been, it would not be enough, he realized, to make this place his home.

Home for Samuel meant waking up and going to sleep by the light of the menorah, wearing the garments of a high priest and attending a sacrifice offered on behalf of the children of Israel, listening to people who were seeking either answers or an argument with the high priest, and putting up with Issachar's sarcasm. Such events had shaped two thirds of his life. And he knew, with just as much certainty, that things would never be that way again.

Not that he missed everything about those days. Samuel did not long for a return of Hophni's cold, calculating ambition or of

Phinehas's crude bullying. He had lost sleep during those days as well, but he had done so to help Eli prepare for the annual Day of Atonement. But as hard as he tried to sort it out he honestly didn't know whether it was because life at the sanctuary was simply what he'd gotten used to, or that he truly felt that the Lord had meant for him to be there and no place else.

But if that were true, why had He let the sanctuary fall?

The boy bowed his head in the darkness and asked the Lord to give him an answer.

It didn't come.

Beginning to feel the cold of the evening, he rose and started back into the house. He wasn't halfway across the compound when a thought did occur to him: the name of a person. But he had no idea when or how he could get word to that individual. Still, he told himself that he would find a way.

★　★　★

As the days became longer and warmer, the mood changed on the farmstead. Life didn't become any easier. On the contrary, the pace of work picked up. Still, life became more good-natured, even festive.

The first crop to ripen was the barley. A hardy crop, it flourished in soils where others would not, yielding two to three hundredfold. Unfortunately, it was not as versatile or desirable as wheat. When ground into flour and baked, barley yielded a coarse and heavy bread. It was what people survived on until the wheat harvest, and it was only the more desperately poor who gleaned the barley fields belonging to others. If anyone gleaned Elkanah's barley, Samuel never knew about it.

The weeks went on, and the wheat ripened in the field. A festive atmosphere settled on the land during the wheat harvest. It meant the closing of part of the harvest cycle, though part of it may have been simple anticipation of eating something other than barley.

It was a clear and warm day when Samuel accompanied Elkanah and the sons of Peninah to harvest the wheat. The good mood of the season had affected them all, especially the brothers who by some providence had made no jests at Samuel's expense for several days. The family's attention had focused on someone else.

The someone in this case was Lebiya, who, rumors said, had managed to catch the eye of a boy several years older than she from a nearby farm. Izhar and Zaccur were merciless in their teasing and predicted that nothing would come of it, but Shemed was oddly silent, perhaps because he himself was looking to marry a girl from yet another farmstead. Samuel had heard Peninah state that even though it meant having to scrape together a dowry for Lebiya, it also meant that Shemed would acquire a dowry, so things would even out and might even end up in their favor. Family talk centered on the possibility as they went into the field.

"You think someone will actually take Lebiya?" Shemed asked.

"Only if he's not in his right mind," Izhar replied.

"If he does, what will happen to us?" Shemed continued.

"What do you mean?"

"I mean, Mother has her doing a lot of the work. Who'll do it in her place?"

"Why not Samuel?"

"That's right—he looks halfway like a girl already!"

Samuel's face flushed. Although his return home after Eli's death had effectively ended his obligation to observe the Nazirite vow, he had never cut his long hair, nor had he allowed anyone else to trim it. And he had not yet started to grow any facial hair.

"We're here," Elkanah said. "Let's get started."

With that, Peninah's sons started harvesting while Elkanah instructed Samuel how to do it. He gave Samuel a sickle, a curved wooden implement set with flint teeth along the inside of the curve.

"Grab a handful of the stalks like this," he said. "Not too close to the top, but not so low to the ground, either."

"About here?" Samuel asked.

"That's right. Cut the stalks about there, just below where you're grasping them. Then when you've collected enough stalks— I'll show you how many is enough—you bundle them into a sheaf. Then we'll take them out to be threshed."

Because Elkanah was working with Samuel, the half brothers didn't try to harass him. In fact, everything seemed to go fairly well that day, and they had the harvest finished just before midday. They had just started gathering up whatever sheaves they could each carry when Shemed asked, "Father, shall I chase them off?"

In a corner of the field, one where Samuel had been working, two women and a man appeared to be continuing to harvest in spite of the gathering heat of the day. Before Elkanah could answer, however, Samuel said, "No, leave them alone."

The brothers turned on him, massing like a storm cloud over the sea.

"What did you say?" Shemed asked slowly.

"I said to leave them alone. They're gleaning."

"And that makes it all right to steal our food without working for it themselves?" Although his voice was controlled, everyone could sense the anger in his voice.

"But it *is* work. They glean because they're poor."

"And that's supposed to be *our* problem?"

"Shemed, it's a good crop this year; let it go," Elkanah said, but it was as if his son didn't hear.

"It's not a problem," Samuel went on, starting to back away, "but it's our duty to let them."

"That's it!" Shemed shouted as he swung his sickle at Samuel. "Let's see how well you can boss us around after I've slit your throat!"

Elkanah made a grab for Shemed's arm, but his son easily shook him off. Shemed took a swing at Samuel, who managed to duck back in time. Finally Elkanah managed to get a better grip on Shemed, and his brothers joined in trying to restrain him while Samuel stood frozen with fear. The boy looked for some place to run to, then saw Lebiya racing toward them. Something about her face made Samuel suddenly feel cold all over.

"Go . . . the house . . . ," she panted. "Someone's asking for you . . . now!"

Welcoming the opportunity to escape, Samuel dashed toward the house. He didn't stop running until he was close enough to see a man pacing just in front of the entrance to the courtyard. When he saw the expression on the stranger's face he stopped. It reminded him too much of the man who had told Eli of the death of his sons and of the capture of the ark.

"Are you the seer?" he asked.

Samuel nodded.

"You must come. Hurry!"

"Where? Why?"

"Beth-Shemesh."

"What happened?"

"Please, just come!"

There was no arguing with the urgency in the man's voice. They started down the road at once.

★   ★   ★

It was more than a day's journey from Ramah to Beth-Shemesh. They traveled east through Gibeon and Kiriath-Jearim before descending toward the coastal plain. Beth-Shemesh nestled in the foothills just below the highlands. That meant it was perilously close to the coastal plain captured and occupied by the Sea People.

Samuel's first thought was that the invaders had done something, either that they'd attacked another city or taken prisoners. He tried to ask the man he was traveling with, whose name he discovered was Shelah, what had happened, but the man seemed to be too much in shock to do anything but keep walking. Shelah didn't stop until, practically at the end of his strength, he paused where the road forked in a clearing and led to the Aijalon Valley. By now the light had begun to fade, and the land around them began to lose its color.

"We can stop here," Shelah said, his voice hoarse, "and continue in the morning."

"What happened? Did someone ask for me?"

Shelah nodded. "They remembered you from the tabernacle, knew you were in Ramah." He pulled his clothes tighter around him. "They said you'd know."

"Know what?" But the man had already fallen asleep.

Sighing, Samuel studied his surroundings. It wasn't the prospect of sleeping outdoors that bothered him. Lambing time had given him a taste of what that was going to be like. Nor was he worried about the weather. The sky was clear, with no hint of the latter rains that came in the spring—rains that, like a child's mood, could shift from angry or sad or joyful from one moment to the next.

What bothered him as he looked around the deserted hill country with its dense evergreen *maquis,* or thickets of lentisk bushes, carob trees, Kermes oaks, terebinth thickets, and stands of tall Alleppo pines, was the fact that he still didn't know what he had been summoned for. Shelah had volunteered nothing aside from a few incoherent mutterings before going to sleep. And it was an open question as to whether he would say anything the next morning. Samuel couldn't guess as to what he would find—he could only wait. After asking the Lord's protection through the evening, he built a small fire to discourage any animals from approaching. Then he lay down as well and eventually slept.

"We must hurry!" Shelah urged as he shook him awake several hours later. Most of the stars had faded from the sky, which had shifted from black to shades of dark blue. Dawn was still some time off, but Shelah seemed in a hurry to be on his way.

"We must hurry!" the man repeated as Samuel slowly got to his feet. "Before there are any more . . ."

"Any more what?"

"Just . . . hurry!" Shelah said as he started east again, with Samuel trying to catch up and wake up at the same time.

It was just before the sun emerged above the hills behind them that Samuel first saw it through a gap in the vegetation, spread out along the east like a monster threatening to swallow all of the world. It was the sea.

Samuel had seen the Jordan River when he and Abdon had gone to collect a bullock from Zeeb. Although most of his memories from that time had faded like grass in late summer, he still remembered the river—its width, its power, its sense of eternity. The sea before him was all that and a hundredfold more. Samuel had heard stories of the Sea People and had figured half of them to be exaggerations. Now he paused. Any people who could conquer something as vast as the sea could be stopped only by the power of God.

Shelah seemed to take no notice as he started down a path, as sure of his steps as a mountain goat. Samuel followed along, careful as to his footing.

By the time the sun had risen high enough to slant through the treetops Samuel could see what appeared to be a fortified town ahead of them. That, he told himself, must be Beth-Shemesh. Then he noticed Shelah glancing back at him and shaking his head.

"This way," he said to Samuel, "in the fields."

To their right, Samuel saw a vast field of wheat, rippling in the breeze like the waves of the sea in the distance. But he noticed something else as well. Although people filled the field, they weren't harvesting. They had gathered near the road Shelah and Samuel now followed. Then Samuel caught a sound, one that chilled him in spite of the warm sun on his face. It was the wailing of mourners.

Shelah suddenly sprinted forward, as if forgetting Samuel was even there. The boy trotted behind, but froze in his tracks when he caught up with him.

Just off the road, lying on the edge of the wheat field, arrayed like flax stalks left to dry in the sun, sprawled dozens of bodies. They were mostly men, some stripped down to their skirtlike undergarments to work. In addition, they included some youths as well, and even a couple boys no older than Samuel himself. All were dead.

"You came," someone said. Samuel turned around and faced Keilah, the former priest who had sheltered him in his one-room house months ago in Ramah. "You really came." His voice was flat, and his eyes had a dazed look.

"What happened?"

"I came here because they needed harvesters. I had to do something—we were so far in debt. Rekem, another Levite whom I remembered from Shiloh, told me I could find work here, so I came. I started laboring yesterday morning in the field. Everything was going well until . . ."

He stopped, then as if he'd fallen from the sky, he dropped to the ground and started sobbing in agony. Samuel looked around. Nobody stepped up to comfort Keilah, mainly because they also were convulsed with grief. Finally Samuel sat on the dusty ground, placed a hand on Keilah's shoulder, and waited. After a minute or so the Levite pulled himself together.

"It was the strangest thing that any of us had ever seen. There were two cows—milk cows, from the look of them—drawing a cart. They were just walking down the road, as if everything was perfectly ordinary. But when the cart got closer . . ."

"What?"

In answer, Keilah pointed to a corner of the field where another small knot of people had gathered. Samuel walked over, and as he neared the people, the low murmur of voices suddenly ceased. Then they parted, and Samuel saw what they were surrounding. An improvised patchwork of outer cloaks had been thrown over it. But there was no mistaking what it was—the ark of the covenant. Stunned, Samuel returned to Keilah.

"When we saw that the ark had been returned, everyone forgot about harvesting," the Levite continued. "They started throwing their cloaks on the ground in front of it. People were summoned from the village. We were . . . we were so happy . . .

"Then we discussed what we should do. The first thing we decided was to offer a sacrifice. So we slaughtered the two milk cows and sacrificed them to the Lord, after taking the cart apart to use its wood for the fire. That's when we noticed the other box as well."

"What box?" Samuel asked, fearful as to the answer.

In response, one of the young men who had gathered around Samuel and Keilah handed the boy a small gold chest. "This was in the wagon," he explained, "next to the ark." Samuel examined it. The design and craftsmanship were foreign to him. When he started to open it, people screamed or gasped and started backing away. He looked back toward the ark, then at the chest. This felt different from the ark, but not threatening. Finally he removed the lid.

Inside the small chest nestled 10 golden objects. Five were fine castings of what appeared to be mice. The other five appeared at first to be mere lumps, but Samuel recognized them instantly as resembling the skin tumors he had seen in vision. Closing the chest, he turned to Keilah.

"This was all that was with the ark?"

"Yes. The Sea People must have put it on the cart when they sent back the ark. But why?"

"I think I know." Samuel's voice was strong, calm, and steady. "How many cities have they captured?"

"Well, they've occupied the major cities of Aphek, Ekron, Ashdod, Gath, and Ashkelon."

"Then that's where they took the ark, to each of those cities.

And in every one of them the judgment of God fell upon them."

"On *them!*" a woman shouted, her face streaked with tears. "What about us? Why did the Lord bring this upon us, His own people?"

"She's right!" someone shouted as other people in the crowd started echoing her anger. "The Sea People have turned our God against us!"

"They cursed the ark!"

"What did we do to deserve this?"

"You *know* what you did!" Samuel shouted back. His words were so loud and angry that the people immediately backed away. "You most of all! How many of you were at Shiloh as I was? How many of you rejoiced when Hophni and Phinehas seized the ark from the tabernacle? Too many of you. I remember! You thought the ark was a talisman, some piece of magic you could do with as you pleased against whomever you pleased. You thought you could tell the Lord what to do instead of seeking in His law for what *He* wanted *you* to do! The Sea People had nothing to do with this. It was your own pride, your own disobedience, that brought this judgment upon us!"

Samuel felt as if his blood was boiling in his ears. The words burst from him. A fire blazed inside him that found release only when he spoke. And the Lord wasn't giving him the words so much as the fire behind them.

"You're Levites, many of you! You *knew* that the ark was a sacred thing, not something to dance around like the golden calf in the wilderness of Sinai! Or did you think that it didn't matter anymore with Shiloh gone and Eli dead? Didn't you think *anything* mattered anymore?"

An uneasy silence spread over them for a long time, during which Samuel could only hear his heart beating strong and fast. Then toward the back of the crowd he heard a woman begin to cry softly. As the sobbing grew louder others joined in. It did not resemble the wails he had heard as he had first approached them and seen the bodies lying in the field. These people were mourning not the loss of a loved one or of a friend, but the destruction of their own illusions. They knew—they knew in their hearts—that they had sinned.

And as they shook with grief, Samuel dropped to his own knees and began to cry as well. He wept, not for any one person among the dead, but for all of those living who surrounded him. His sobs were a lament for all Israel, now as helpless as a small child, contending against the Sea People and even death itself. And he anguished for those who could not, would not, learn what the Lord had sought to teach them in the most striking way possible.

As Samuel's grief subsided he glanced up into the tear-streaked faces of those surrounding him. Something about the way they stared at him was a little unsettling. He had seen that look before when he had helped decide cases at the gate in Ramah and had been thanked by the one in whose favor he had ruled. It was an expression of gratitude and also something more. It both humbled and frightened him. Then Keilah stepped forward, his hands folded as one begging. "Please, tell us what to do."

Samuel wiped his eyes with the back of one hand and stood. He surveyed the rapt faces of those surrounding him and asked, "Does anyone have a barn?"

★   ★   ★

Among those working in the field that day were people from Kiriath-Jearim, through which Samuel had passed on his way to Beth-Shemesh. They agreed to return and see if that village would consent to accept custody of the ark, as Samuel wanted to take it back up to the highlands, in case the Sea People should be tempted to seize it again. As they waited for word from Kiriath-Jearim, the people of Beth-Shemesh set about the task of burying their dead. Fully 70 people had perished, leaving few families unaffected.

Toward the end of the day a message arrived that the inhabitants of Kiriath-Jearim had agreed to assume responsibility for the ark. In the interim, as if sure of the decision, Samuel had sought among the people for anyone who was a Levite and commanded them to go home and get their old linen robes if they still had them.

It was a solemn and strange procession that made their way up through the foothills toward Kiriath-Jearim. The ark, now covered by a large cloth instead of a motley collection of outer garments, led the way, carried on poles by Levites as the law commanded. Samuel with others from Beth-Shemesh followed at a respectful distance.

When they approached the village Samuel spoke with Abinadab, an older man who had volunteered to store the ark at his place. "Do you have a son?" Samuel asked.

"Yes, his name is Eleazar."

"I want to see him. And bring me some oil."

Abinadab wasn't sure why Samuel wanted the oil, but he called for his son, and soon the young man stood before the boy holding a small clay bottle of olive oil.

The crowd looked on as Samuel anointed Eleazar. "From this moment on, it is your responsibility to make sure nothing happens to the ark of the covenant, that nobody disturbs it and that no damage comes to it."

"I understand. But . . ."

"What?"

"For how long?"

"I'll tell you when. It may be a long time."

"You mean a year?"

"It could be 20 years, for all I know. Whenever the Lord says the time has come for it to go elsewhere, I'll notify you."

Abinadab's "barn" was really no more than a generous storage room attached to the outside of his house with only one exterior door. The people installed the ark there with as much solemnity as they could summon at a moment's notice. Samuel tore a patch from the hem of his garment and fastened it to the door of the building with a handful of mud from around a nearby trough. "I'll be coming back to check that this seal is unbroken," he declared, and nobody questioned that he would.

Abinadab offered his house to Samuel that he might stay the night. The food was no different than the fare he had become used to at Ramah, but it seemed to taste better by the absence of constant tension as his host's family sat and ate as one instead of the two warring armies that Elkanah's family had become.

Suddenly Samuel realized just how tired and hungry he was. It was as if the Lord had kept him going until he had arranged safekeeping for the ark, and only now was he aware of what he had been through. Feeling as empty as a bottomless jar, he managed to mumble an apology to Abinadab before dropping into a heavy, dreamless sleep.

The following morning he left Kiriath-Jearim. But he did not go home.

★   ★   ★

Turning north just short of Ramah, Samuel followed the road through Mizpah and Beth-El until, as he neared Lebonah, he headed east and walked up the familiar valley where less than a year ago the tabernacle had stood. Avoiding the place, he journeyed north up a short valley and arrived at midday at the small town of Shiloh. Finding the potter's house, he paused in front of it. It had been less than a year since he had been there. Had anything changed since then? Hesitantly he knocked on the door.

No response.

As he prepared to knock again he heard a voice from inside. "Go away! We don't want the business of anyone crazy enough to be out at this time of day!"

"Issachar!"

Samuel heard a shuffling inside and the sound of clay jars being knocked together. Then the door flew open. There stood Issachar, his smile as alive as his eyes were dead.

Inside the shop pottery of some kind took up almost every inch of space. Samuel immediately started telling Issachar what had happened at Beth-Shemesh, leaving nothing out. The blind potter was silent for a long time.

"So," he finally said, "the ark is safe. And how about you?"

"What?"

Issachar shook his head. "Why is it that you have the eyes and I'm the only one who can see? You don't know what happened out there, do you?"

"To all those people?"

"No, to you! You told me that you anointed what's-his-name, Eleazar? Did you ever think that *you've* been anointed too?"

"Well, no, not at the moment. I only said what had to be said, what . . . what the Lord wanted me to say." The boy's voice grew quieter as he spoke. "But I didn't plan it . . ."

"And you didn't plan on going to Beth-Shemesh either, I imagine."

"No."

"You're still serving the Lord, boy, but not the way you did when Eli was alive. And after today you'd better get used to being called 'seer.'"

"But . . ."

"So," Issachar continued as if nothing out of the ordinary had happened, "what's your family like?"

Almost with a sense of relief, Samuel began to regale Issachar with his account of life with Elkanah, Peninah, Hannah, and their respective children. He also told them about farm life and his own doubts about his competence.

"Take my advice, boy: don't work too hard at this farming business. About the only thing it's good for, aside from filling your belly, is helping you understand what farmers go through. And you're no farmer, no matter what anybody says. The Lord's meant you for something else."

"That's what I've been telling myself, but this isn't what I expected."

"I didn't expect to be spending my days up to my elbows in wet clay, either, but that's what the Lord did for me. With some help."

"Thanks, Issachar."

"So are you going home now?"

"It's too late to start for home at the moment."

"Well, if you can find it, I may have an open corner around here where you can sleep."

"I'd like that," Samuel said. Even Issachar could sense the boy's smile.

Unlike the previous night at the home of Ahitophel, it was late when Samuel lay down to sleep. He and Issachar had talked and reminisced until long after sunset, and for the first time since returning to Ramah he drifted off to sleep feeling as if he'd come one step closer to home. And it wasn't just that he was with Issachar, but because of what the potter had told him.

The following day Samuel arrived in Ramah in the afternoon as Elkanah and his sons were threshing grain. Elkanah immediately dropped the large wooden fork he was using to separate the grain from the stalks and chaff and ran to the boy, embracing him.

"Typical," Shemed muttered. "We're back here slaving away, and who gets the big welcome?"

"So what have you been doing all this time?" Izhar called out.

Samuel looked toward him and with perfect calmness said: "What the Lord meant for me to do. I had to start by helping to bury 70 people struck dead in Beth-Shemesh."

"What?" Elkanah asked. "But how did they die?"

Samuel glanced at his brothers, said "I don't exactly know," then went inside to greet his mother.

Part Two

IN THE 10 YEARS SINCE HIS return from Shiloh Samuel had learned to be a pretty fair farmer, but that was about as good as he ever got. His older brothers were still stronger than he was and more adept at doing the physical work that agriculture required. They also had a better sense and knowledge of its practical details—the reading of the sky, the judging of the soil, the condition of the animals.

Their knowledge and skill made Elkanah proud, but it also left the sons of Peninah with a sense of superiority. Elkanah could no longer keep up with the four young men as they worked, and was glad enough to entrust the labor of the farm to them whenever he could. The sons, however, took it a step further, speaking of the place among themselves as *their* farm and thinking of Elkanah more as a hired hand than as their father. Of course, they never spoke or acted that way in his presence.

Nor did they take any of Elkanah's other children into account, except as additional farm laborers—especially in the case of Samuel.

For his part, though, Samuel didn't mind one way or the other.

Through the years Elkanah and especially Hannah had encouraged him to be patient with himself and to learn the ways of farming. He did so, but he also remembered the words of Issachar: that farming was just something for him to do until the Lord spoke to him again or otherwise made His purpose known.

And that's what Samuel did. He took his turn behind the plow, helped sow the wheat and barley and flax seeds, and assisted during lambing time. But he also spent time at the city gate at Ramah, leaving his work at a moment's notice if someone showed up at the house asking for his help. It was more than simply being glad for any chance to get away from the sons of Peninah. Somehow it always felt right when he was at the gate, steering people through their own arguments toward a destination of which they could both approve, or of calling to the memory of the people listening to him the words of the Lord. He had become so sure, so certain that it was what the Lord meant for him to do that he pretty much stopped listening to the taunts of his older half brothers. They had told him that he would never amount to anything as a farmer. Samuel found himself agreeing with them, which turned out to be enough to end a lot of quarrels before they even started.

As word of what had happened at Beth-Shemesh spread throughout the highlands, Samuel's reputation also increased. Because he was not a Levite, he was not eligible to be a high priest himself and thus a successor to Eli. Even if one of the high priest's sons had been alive, there was still no sanctuary to which he could return. Israel no longer had a central place of worship, and there was no hurry to reestablish it at Shiloh or anywhere else.

But if the nation no longer had a sanctuary or high priest, there remained a need for people to fix their spiritual longings and hopes upon some individual. Through the years the Lord raised up a number of such *shoftim,* or "judges," in Israel. They were a strange collection of people: Ehud, son of Gera, the left-handed assassin of Eglon, king of Moab; Deborah, a woman prophet and military leader; Gideon, a farmer turned military strategist; Jephthah, a soldier whose rashness had meant the death of his daughter; and Samson, whose heroism and strength barely outstripped his lust.

And now people were accepting Samuel as a judge. It was not a position that he had sought, but one for which the Lord had prepared him, first by bringing him into the world when it appeared that Hannah would be forever barren, then by having him grow up at the sanctuary at Shiloh, where his childhood had been steeped in the rituals given to Israel through Moses. This much Samuel had come to accept.

Beyond that, however, he was not yet sure exactly what the Lord wanted from him. In the case of the other *shoftim* there seemed to be no doubt. Israel had had external enemies to subdue, such as the Moabites or the Sea People. Was Samuel to seek out and destroy as they had? Something in his heart, whether it was the Lord or not, told him that this wasn't what God had called him for. Not at the moment, anyway.

For the present, his duties had been to render judgment at the gate at Ramah, which during the past few years had become more and more crowded as Samuel's fame grew. It wasn't long before he had become known for his scrupulous honesty as much as for his wisdom and knowledge of the law. His reputation grew in proportion to Peninah's resentment at his refusal to accept payment from any party after he had rendered a judgment.

"I just can't say no to anyone who wants my help," he told her one evening as the family gathered for their evening meal. "If they need my help, then it's my duty to go."

"And what about your duty to us?" she snapped. "The crops don't harvest themselves."

"I help!" Ahitub protested.

"How much help can we expect from a 10-year-old?"

"Credit where it's due," Izhar smirked. "He's still more capable of work around here than Samuel."

"You take that back!"

"Ahitub!" Samuel said, momentarily forgetting about Peninah. "Remember what you promised."

"I remember," he sulked as he sat back down. Izhar didn't say anything, but a part of him was relieved. For even at 10 years old, it was clear that Ahitub was developing into a capable fighter, as ready as Lebiya had ever been. He lacked the strength to hit solidly, but everyone could sense that he had potential. Also he tended to grab an opponent in a fight, even if it was one of his big brothers, and hang on like Jacob wrestling with the angel. The sons of Peninah could still use their advantages of size and strength, but they knew that the boy would grow to be a serious opponent soon enough. So they refrained from speaking against Samuel, not because they had finally come to respect what he had become, but because they didn't want to condition Ahitub to turn against them.

But Peninah clung to the topic like a scavenger dog with a bone. "And now we're going to lose another worker because you insist on

Ahitub's going with you," she sputtered.

"Not if he doesn't behave himself," Samuel replied, glancing at the boy. But a light in Samuel's eyes assured Ahitub he didn't have to worry about being left behind. Still, the boy knew that he'd better watch his tongue until they were on the road.

"Peninah, we've been through all this before," Elkanah said as patiently as possible. "Samuel will be going only after the wheat harvest. There's not much to do then except tend the grapevines."

"When are we going?" Ahitub asked excitedly.

"As Father said, when the harvest is finished."

"Hope you like hot weather," Izhar taunted.

"I don't mind hot weather," Ahitub answered, a touch of bravado in his voice. "I won't even mind if we see any of the Sea People!"

"Not much chance of that happening," Samuel said. "We're only going to—"

"I know!" he said eagerly. "We're going to Gilgal, Bethel, and . . . Mizpah!"

"Very good," Samuel smiled.

" 'Very good.' He only says the names of those places 50 times a day!" Shemed snorted.

"Samuel," Hannah asked, "do you really think it's wise to take him along with you?"

"I'm only doing what he asked. He wants to know what I do and how I do it when I travel to the other Benjaminite cities every year."

"The gossip of old men!" Shemed muttered.

"It's not gossip."

"It doesn't matter to me what it is," Izhar added as he pointed to Samuel. "I know what I'd do if I was in his position."

"You'd fall asleep from drinking too much," Lebiya said acidly.

"That's enough, Lebiya," Elkanah said, but he had to work at suppressing a smile when she'd said it. As for Ahitub, he laughed heartily.

The family dropped the subject, and soon most of them went off to their various sleeping quarters. Hannah, however, approached Samuel. "Are you sure about this," she asked, "that there won't be any danger?"

"Mother, I honestly don't see any danger, and the Lord hasn't shown any to me. Do you think I'd take Ahitub with me if the Lord had revealed to me otherwise?"

She smiled. "Then I'm content."

★　★　★

The warm southern winds had not yet arrived when Samuel and Ahitub began preparing for their travels. Hurling in from the desert across the Salt Sea, the wind blasted the ground and baked it like pottery, leaving the soil impossible to work until the arrival of the early rains. While the winds didn't seem to have anything in common with the winter rains, both could bring farming to a dead halt. Which was one reason the family could "spare" Samuel to make the rounds when they did not have as much to do in the high summer.

Then, too, there was the fact that he was needed—or at least they requested his presence—at the three cities. Samuel sometimes found it hard to believe that all three cities lacked someone who could arbitrate claims or cite the law of Moses when the occasion arose. It also sometimes crossed his mind that his being asked to judge may have been nothing more than an excuse for some to boast of Samuel's presence afterward, but he tried not to think about it too much. The important thing was his role as judge, not his status.

Still he was glad for any excuse to get away from the house. Summer was an oppressive time in a way that was different from winter. In winter the struggle was to stay warm and dry, even as rain found ways to enter a house through the walls and ceiling. Still, a house afforded a measure of shelter unavailable in the open.

It was different in the summer. Like a persistent fly, the heat from outdoors crept indoors and became just as bothersome. The typical home had no real window except for a small opening high in the wall, and leaving the doorway open provided little or no relief. Despite the fact that people built their homes with the doorways facing north in order to avoid the harshest sunlight, a house could become as hot as an oven after a time. Even the extreme measure of opening a hole in the roof offered no real solution, as it only traded heat for more sunlight.

All things considered, it was better to be on the road during those days, even for small journeys of less than a day's travel. And, Samuel reflected, the excitement of his young companion would make the journey even more interesting.

Samuel's other siblings had all been born and were growing up while he was at Shiloh, which may have had something to do with the fact that he felt closer to Ahitub than to the others. He certainly didn't dislike any of them, but having spent the past 10 years watching Ahitub develop from infancy to childhood was something that Samuel had never experienced in his time at Shiloh. While the community had had other children there of varying ages, he had rarely seen or interacted with them. He had mainly stayed with Eli, aside from whatever time he spent with Issachar.

It was therefore as much of an education for Samuel to watch Ahitub's development as it was for the boy himself. Elkanah and the sons of Peninah didn't pay as close attention to child rearing because they felt that it was the province of women. Besides, they had enough to do already. To them a child like Ahitub was a laborer-in-training, someone who wasn't all that interesting in their own right and who certainly wouldn't be useful until they learned the skills they needed. It was enough work to keep the farm going, and everything else just wasn't their problem.

Samuel understood their perspective, but couldn't bring himself to agree. Elkanah and the others may have spent their time studying the cultivation and growth of wheat and flax, of olive trees and grape vines, but for Samuel the maturation of Ahitub was equally as gripping. He had studied the boy's developmental landmarks, from standing to walking to talking, as intently as he had listened to Eli discoursing on the law.

The major difference, of course, was that the law never answered back when you studied it. To interact with Ahitub, to listen to his attempts to talk and then to reply, to hold his hands as he took those initial uncertain steps . . . something about it transcended what Samuel felt about his role as seer. Not that he was ever interested in abandoning that responsibility—after all this time, it would have been unthinkable as well as a betrayal of the trust the Lord had put in him when He had started communicating with Samuel. But it brought a certain enjoyment to his life to know that Ahitub was part of it.

Lebiya emerged from the house carrying a dried goatskin. From the way she carried it—balancing it as if its contents shifted from one end to the other—Samuel guessed that Hannah had provided them with soured goat's milk to drink. Fairly soon, he knew, the summer winds would dry up the few remaining springs on the highlands.

"Here," she said as she handed the skin to Samuel, who tied it onto the donkey they'd be using. "Wish I was going with you."

Samuel paused in tying the knot. "Really?"

"Really. And I'm not just saying that because I'd rather be doing anything else than helping Peninah with the housework. Which is true enough!"

"I don't know. It could get kind of boring. Isn't that right, Ahitub?"

"No, it won't!" the boy said emphatically.

"Well, be sure and tell us what happened when you get back," she said. "Even the boring parts."

"I always do," Samuel said, "no matter what your brothers have to say about it."

"They're your brothers too, you know."

"Just like me?" Ahitub asked.

"No, it's . . . different," Samuel said absentmindedly.

"How is it different?"

Lebiya smiled. "You'd better get going. You've got a lot of questions to answer."

"Not just yet," Samuel said. "I still need to get something from Mother."

He then entered the house where his brothers were still finishing up breakfast. Samuel and Ahitub had eaten earlier in order to pack. The brothers ignored Samuel, and he preferred it that way. Hannah rose and handed a small woven bag to him. As he hefted it, the bag felt light, and he could feel small objects rolling around inside.

"Those better not be the last of the raisins," Zaccur said, even though his mouth was full of bread.

"They're not," Hannah said simply.

"Besides," Samuel said, in spite of not wanting to talk to them, "the new crop will be ready in a few more months."

"No thanks to you," Shemed muttered.

Samuel paused. *Let it go,* he told himself. *He doesn't really want to talk—he wants to fight. And he wants to do it with words.*

So Samuel kissed Hannah goodbye, assured her for the thousandth time that he and Ahitub would be fine, then without a word to the brothers left the house. Once outside, he tied the bag of raisins to the bundle hanging off the donkey's right flank.

"Ready?" Samuel asked.

Ahitub nodded.

Samuel bent down and effortless lifted the boy off the ground, swung him around, and placed him on the donkey's back. Taking hold of the rope that served as a bridle, he started off.

★   ★   ★

It wasn't far between Ramah and Bethel, the first stop on Samuel's annual itinerary. After a while they would move on to Gilgal, then Mizpah, and finally back home to Ramah.

An old feeling haunted Samuel as he thought about that. Even 10 years after the fall of the sanctuary, he *still* had to convince himself that "home" meant Ramah. It just didn't feel right.

"Samuel?"

"What is it?" He glanced over his shoulder at the boy.

"May I walk a little? My legs hurt." He did look uncomfortable, straddling a loaded donkey.

"All right." Samuel tried to stop the donkey, but the animal wasn't in a very cooperative mood. It kept plodding along, heedless of both Samuel tugging at the rope and of the boy's laughter. But the donkey soon got the message and halted, and Samuel lifted Ahitub off the animal's back. In a second they were walking down the road, Ahitub's hand resting on the bundles hanging from one side of the donkey.

"Watch out for the knots. We don't want any of them to come untied yet."

"All right. Samuel?"

"Yes?"

"Where'd you learn to tie these knots?"

"I really didn't learn until I came back here. It wasn't something I had to know at the sanctuary."

"What did you have to learn?"

"I told you already—about the sacrifices and offerings and about the law of Moses, and so on."

"Was that all?"

"Mainly. I must have learned some other things as well, but I can't remember what they are. Other people took care of a lot of the things that happened there. Some made tents, others pottery, a few worked in gold—"

"What was that like?"

"I never got there too often, but one man, Chisda the goldsmith, did all the goldsmithing. He was good. Chisda could take a piece of gold, hammering it again and again until it looked like . . ."

"Like what?"

In answer Samuel reached up to his forehead, worked to find one hair between his thumb and forefinger, then gave it a tug. Then he handed it to Ahitub. "Like that—just that long and just that fine."

"Wow!" Then, "What would you need gold like that for?"

"For weaving. We used gold thread in the tapestries inside the tabernacle, the curtain at the entrance of the courtyard, and the clothes of the high priest."

"Did you have gold threads in your clothes?"

"No," Samuel admitted. "My clothes weren't exactly like the high priest's."

"Where are they?"

Samuel stopped. "Where are what?" he asked cautiously.

"Your clothes. Did you bring them home with you?"

"I . . . I was wearing only a linen robe when I returned home. I don't know what happened to the rest. And the linen robe probably got used up for lamp wicks years ago."

"*Lamp* wicks?"

"Well, that's what happened to the old robes of the high priest when they became so worn that they had to be replaced. The robe was cut up into little pieces and the pieces twisted up and put into the menorah as wicks."

"Oh."

Samuel detected a note of dejection and disappointment in Ahitub's single word response. Although Samuel had described the garments a thousand times before to the boy, this was the first time that Ahitub had ever asked about them. It was also the first time that Samuel realized that he didn't want Ahitub to know what had really happened to his garments. Uncomfortable with the subject, he let it drop and instead pointed out the crossroad they were approaching. Turning north, they continued on toward Bethel.

It wasn't long before Samuel and Ahitub could see Bethel ahead of them. Samuel would pitch his tent outside the precincts of the city, as he would at the other two cities on his itinerary. In this Ahitub proved to be a real help. At 10 years old he was already as tall as Samuel had been when he was 12. They had the tent set up in time for their mid-day rest. As excited as Ahitub had been when they had been traveling, he dropped off to sleep almost immediately. Samuel kept watch. He wasn't looking out for wild animals, however, but for people.

His circuit had been established for only a few years, but he had learned some important lessons from the first few times. For instance, he had discovered that it was best to send word ahead to each of the cities that he was coming and that he would *not* see anyone except at the gate. If effect, he was stating in advance that he would accept food and shelter from no one lest that person be a party in a case he would hear. And judges, he repeatedly said, had to be indebted to nobody if they wished to remain impartial.

Nobody seemed to be approaching his tent. That was understandable since nobody in their right mind would be out at midday anyway. Confident that they would not be disturbed for a while, he entered the tent himself and was soon asleep.

★   ★   ★

Bethel was a city with a venerable history. Abraham had once camped here and had built an altar, seeking God's counsel and offering sacrifices. Here, too, Jacob had stopped while on the run from his brother Esau. Here he had slept and dreamed of angels traveling between heaven and earth. But today neither dreams of angels or of anything else disturbed Samuel's sleep.

When he awoke several hours later he saw Ahitub already sitting up and looking intently outside.

"Is someone coming?" Samuel asked. Ahitub nodded and pointed toward two figures approaching the tent from the city. They appeared to be master and servant, for one of them looked fairly prosperous while the other one, carrying a burden of some kind, was dressed more simply.

"They're starting early," Samuel muttered. "But the day's too far gone to do anything today."

"Are you going to tell them to go away?"

In answer, Samuel rose and confronted the two men as they neared the tent. Ahitub could now see that the other man carried a bundle of what appeared to be at least three full sets of clothing.

"Are you the seer?" the more prosperous-looking man asked.

"I am Samuel, son of Elkanah. If you're here to seek a judgment, you'll have to wait until tomorrow at the gate."

"Who said anything about a judgment?" the man said with a chuckle. "I saw you camped out here and, as any decent man with a proper roof over his head should, I came to enquire if you might not prefer—"

"I appreciate your concern," Samuel interrupted, "and thank you, but I am all right here. I'm sorry I caused you to come all this way for nothing. Will I see you tomorrow at the gate?"

The man hesitated, which Samuel took to be a yes. "Either way," Samuel continued, "perhaps I may offer you something to eat? We haven't much, but I can spare a bite."

"I wouldn't dream of imposing!" The man had found his tongue quickly enough. "I look forward to . . . hearing you at the gate tomorrow."

"Good day to you, then."

The two men turned and walked away. Samuel went back inside the tent, shaking his head.

"What was that all about?" Ahitub asked.

"It never fails. There's always somebody who thinks he can buy me."

"Buy you? As a slave?"

"Close to one. He wanted to buy my favor, to make sure that if he approached me tomorrow at the gate I would rule in his favor no matter what the facts were."

"Is that what Mother Peninah complains about?"

"Yes," he sighed, "she doesn't seem to realize that an honest judge doesn't do things that way. Or maybe she *does* know and simply doesn't care. I don't know which," he added.

"Did they do that at the tabernacle too?"

"Not really. The tabernacle was mainly a place to offer sacrifices. Most people who came didn't seek a ruling from Eli." He grimaced. "Half the time they just wanted to complain."

"About what?"

"About . . . about his sons."

"Why?"

"They did . . . things . . . that priests weren't supposed to do."

"Such as?"

"It's really not your problem," Samuel said, clearly uncomfortable with the subject. "Nor is it anyone else's problem anymore—with the tabernacle gone."

"Will the Lord ever bring it back?"

"I don't know. He hasn't told *me* anything about it." Samuel managed a weak smile as he said it. "So let's see what we have to eat."

The two of them began to prepare a sparse evening meal of bread, a vegetable stew, and dried fruit with soured goat milk to quench their thirst. Twice more people from Bethel approached Samuel, and twice more he sent them away.

"What did the last man want?" Ahitub asked.

"He didn't want me to give a judgment so much as to prophesy."

"About what?"

"He wanted me to tell his future."

"Oh." Then, "Can you do that?"

Samuel paused for a moment. "Of course I can," he said with a smile. "Want me to show you how?"

"Yeah!"

"Give me your bowl, then."

"What?"

"Your bowl with stew in it—give it to me."

Puzzled, Ahitub handed it to Samuel. "How are you going to tell my future?"

"By looking in the stew."

"Really?"

"I can show you how to do it."

"You *can?*"

"Of course. Now look here," Samuel said as he held the bowl in his palm and rotated it. "You see these cucumber bits floating among the lentils?"

"Yes?"

"Well, how many there are and where they're placed in the bowl represent what kind of future you're going to have. Look, right now there are a good number evenly spread out. They mean a good future, understand?"

"Uh-huh."

"Now," he said as he picked out a number of the cucumber pieces with his fingers and popped them into his mouth, "you still have a good number of pieces, but they're all over on one side. That means your fortune will be sometimes good and sometimes bad. Because it's uneven, you see?"

"I see."

"And this," he said after he'd picked out and eaten almost all of the cucumber, "is a sign of bad fortune—very bad fortune for you."

"How bad? What does it mean?"

"It means somebody's eaten all your cucumbers."

"Hey!"

"Don't worry," Samuel said with a broad grin, "we still have plenty left." He then refilled Ahitub's bowl and handed it back to him. "You angry at me?"

"No. That's a good trick," he said returning the grin. "Where did you learn that, anyway?"

"I just now made it up."

Ahitub couldn't help laughing, even though he had his mouth full.

"Let this be a lesson, Ahitub. Anyone who tells you that they're able to tell the future does that only because you have something that they want: gold, cattle, land . . ."

"Cucumbers?"

"Or cucumbers."

★   ★   ★

Samuel arrived at the gate of Bethel early in the morning. In addition to about a half dozen petitioners who were already waiting for him, there was the usual group of people: men seeking work, vendors laying out their wares, and individuals with nothing better to do.

"Those who have questions about the law will have to wait until after midday," Samuel announced. "Cases requiring judgment will be heard immediately."

Ahitub watched as Samuel decided three cases that morning: the first two involved a boundary dispute hinging on whether stones used as property markers had been moved (because the one against whom the accusation of moving the marker had been brought was reluctant to have him inspect the wall, Samuel found for the other party and specified that a party of men from Bethel would inspect the property and realign the landmarks/stones), and an allegation of theft of an ox ("I knew it was his—I was just keeping it until he came for it"). Samuel ordered the man to hand it over at once since the person who found the lost animal had to take the initiative to return it.

The third case involved the nonpayment of a man who had helped build his neighbor's house.

"And why didn't you pay him what was due him?"

"Because he didn't finish the job!"

"In what way?"

"He neglected to put a parapet around the roof."

"Is this true?" Samuel asked the plaintiff.

"So what if it is? Look at him! He's 80 years old if he's a day. He barely had the strength to come here, let alone climb up on a roof."

"But doesn't the law of Moses command us to respect the elderly?" Samuel's voice had suddenly taken on an edge that brought idle conversation nearby to a halt.

"Yes," the man grudgingly admitted. "But—"

"Do you go up on the roof?" Samuel asked the old man.

"My wife's slave girl does. She was up there two days ago laying out clothes to dry."

Samuel turned to the plaintiff. "Then for the girl's sake, you're obliged to finish the work."

"I have to work myself harder to safeguard the life of a slave?"

"A life is a life! It is the Lord and not you who brings life to be, and it is the Lord and not you who ends it. It's not for you to disregard any life as being of no worth! After all the demands of the law of the Lord, there is no greater obligation laid on anyone than to save a life!"

Samuel had gotten so worked up that he rose from where he'd been seated and started shouting at the man's face. The man backed away in genuine alarm, and an uncomfortable silence descended on the crowd. Samuel stared at the man for a few seconds more, then seemed to realize what he had done. Blushing, he began massaging his forehead.

"Seer, I—" the man stammered, "I will build the parapet around the roof. You don't have to say any more."

"Very well," Samuel replied, sounding exhausted. "It . . . it's almost midday. We'll get something to eat, then rest, and meet here again afterward."

The crowd began to disperse. Earlier there had been an excited, anticipatory tone in the conversation at the gate when Samuel had approached. Now there was just as much discussion, but the tone was hushed, apprehensive, awestruck.

Ahitub studied Samuel's face, but he couldn't tell what his older brother was thinking. If the incident had been something that Samuel had done to impress the people, he had succeeded. Somehow, though, Ahitub got the feeling that this wasn't the case.

"Are you all right?" he asked Samuel, who hadn't spoken a word to him during the walk back to the tent.

"I . . . I had something on my mind, that's all," the older brother answered as he sat down on one of the mats.

"Was it something that God told you?"

"No," Samuel said wearily. "Just never mind. Have something to eat."

"Aren't you hungry?"

"Not really," he said as he lay down to sleep. Ahitub ate only a handful of parched wheat and some raisins, washing it down with soured goat milk before he went to sleep as well. He didn't have much of an appetite either.

The afternoon session wasn't as dramatic. No one had any cases requiring a decision, but a number of people had questions about the law. One man inquired about garments made from a mixture of wool and linen, which was forbidden. Another asked about whether a vow was still binding if the father of the one who took the vow heard of it after it was made but still objected. Other questions dealt with food, animals, houses and lands, slaves and betrothal, and birth and death.

Ahitub watched Samuel throughout the afternoon. His older brother never seemed at a loss for an answer to the problems laid before him. The law appeared to have provisions for *everything,* and Samuel knew them all. It made Ahitub proud to watch him in action.

Yet something troubled him about it as well. As the afternoon went on, Samuel seemed to grow weary of the questions he dealt with, as if each one caused him physical pain. Ahitub could see it in his face.

Finally, with the sun nearing the horizon, Samuel declared the session at an end and stated that if there was anything else that required his attention he would hear it tomorrow morning. Otherwise, he would be moving on to Gilgal and then to Mizpah. Once again, Samuel said nothing as they returned to the tent for the evening meal.

"Are you all right?" Ahitub asked again.

"Why do you keep asking that? Do I look ill?" Samuel managed a half smile.

"You don't look very happy."

"I don't feel very happy."

"Why not? You're doing a good thing, aren't you?"

"Yes, but . . . you wouldn't understand."

"I would too!"

This time Samuel broke out in a full smile. "All right, then. You heard all the questions the people asked?"

"Uh-huh."

"But did you *really* hear them?"

"What do you mean?"

"They weren't interested in the law," Samuel sighed as he sat down to remove a loaf of bread from their bag of provisions. "Only about their problems and what the law has to say about it. And all their questions upon questions: 'Well, what about this?' or 'Well, what about that?'

"The Law of the Lord is important. He gave it to us so that we might know how to live here in the land to which He brought us. But it seems most people think about the law only when it tells them not to do something they want to do, or else to do something they'd rather not do. It was making me tired and . . . and a little angry."

"But they still do it."

"Do what?"

"Think about the law of Moses. Isn't that a good thing?"

Samuel's brow furrowed as he slowly scratched at his beard. Then he glanced at Ahitub and smiled. "You're right. It is a good thing. And even if people would still rather go their own way, that they confront the law at all is a good thing indeed." He reached over and cupped the boy's cheek in one hand while at the same time feeling his own face flushing. "So," he said in what was more like his normal tone of voice, "shall we make some supper?"

"Make a lot—I'm *really* hungry!"

★　★　★

The next morning a good-sized crowd gathered at the gate of Bethel, though pretty much the same people that Ahitub had seen the day before. "Is there a case to be judged?" Samuel asked. Nobody spoke. "Is there a question about the law?" Again, silence.

Ahitub figured all that remained was for Samuel to say goodbye, then they could go back to their tent and pack up everything before leaving for the next city. Instead, Samuel carefully studied each face in the crowd. The crowd was curious, wondering what he would do or say. Then he began speaking:

"Here at Bethel is where our father Jacob stopped as he fled the wrath of his brother, Esau. He had stolen what was his brother's, stolen something he couldn't put in a bag or roll up in a mat. It was the blessing of his father's God, something that the Lord had already promised would be Jacob's, for the Lord had said to Rebekah: 'The older shall serve the younger.' Yet Rebekah, doing what was right in her own eyes, conspired with Jacob to steal what God had promised to her.

"So what could Jacob do? Stay and admit his deceit? It didn't take that long for what had happened to become known. For no matter how skillfully Jacob and Rebekah had conspired to deceive old blind Isaac, they could not keep their actions hidden. In the same way, we have no better chance of hiding our actions and inactions from the one who could tell Cain: 'The voice of your brother's blood cries out to me from the ground.' Isn't it the height of folly to think that we can somehow deceive the one who formed each of us in the womb?

"So Jacob was on the run from the person who had sworn to kill him. From his own brother! And he traveled until he came here. And as the sun had set, he found a rock to rest his head on so he could sleep. Perhaps it was as big as a loaf of leavened bread. Having journeyed all that way with little or no food, how he would have wished that the stone really was a loaf of bread. But just as Esau was undone by a pot full of lentils and spices, so Jacob could do nothing with the blessing he had stolen from Esau to satisfy his own hunger!"

"So Jacob slept here, and he dreamed here. And what did he dream of? He dreamed and saw that even for one such as he, even for one who had broken the law and felt no repentance for what he had done—that even for one who deserved the fate that Esau had planned for him, the Lord still holds open the door of His sanctuary. For he saw the angels of the Lord, the messengers of the Lord, journeying freely between heaven and earth. The Lord who regards us as His children the way He regarded Adam and Eve as His children—the Lord does not turn His back on us, but continually gives us a way to approach Him.

"And what is that way? It is through His law. The law is the first thing God gave to His people when they were finally beyond Pharaoh's reach. The law is what He commanded us to teach each generation that comes after us. The law is one of the sacred objects that resides inside the ark of the covenant.

"But there are those who ask how sacred can it be when even the Sea People can take the ark itself away from us. Yet this is a lie! The Sea People did not capture the ark—it was *given* to them by the sons of Eli. They thought no more of the ark and the law it contained than a woman does a jar of grain that has become infested with mice!

"So as we all know, the sons of Eli perished, and the Sea People took possession of the ark. If you ask a hundred men what happened while the Sea People had the ark in their possession, you will get a hundred answers. For no one knows what truly happened . . . except the one to whom the Lord has revealed it."

At this the people visibly leaned a little closer to Samuel, sure that he was speaking of himself and eager to hear what he would say.

"The Lord showed me the terrible vengeance He brought against the Sea People for their arrogance in thinking that they could make the Lord dance to their tune. It was an arrogance at least as great as that of the sons of Eli. In each of the five great cities to which the Sea People took the ark, cities seized by them from territory that should belong to the children of Jacob, the people suffered the kind of plagues that befell Pharaoh when he refused to hear Moses. First mice overran the fields of the Sea People. Then the Sea People themselves suffered from painful boils. It became so bad that no city wanted anything to do with the ark, and they sent it away.

"And the Lord guided the ark on its return to His people. But what should have been a time of joy turned into an occasion of mourning. For I saw with my own eyes how many of our people fell dead in the fields of Beth-Shemesh. They perished because they were no different than the sons of Eli or the Sea People, each of whom treated the sacred ark and the law it contained as if it was something common. I saw where they had collapsed, lying out in the sun like flax drying on a roof. I saw the looks on their faces, the expressions of terror and fear.

"What makes their deaths so sorrowful is that they in their sin of disrespect for the ark were no different than Jacob and his sin of theft. Had Jacob not deceived his father he need not have run away from home. Had the men of Beth-Shemesh remembered how to respect the ark they need not have died. Their deaths are all the sadder because they need not have happened!"

The crowd at the gate, which had hung on Samuel's every word, now gave vent to their emotions. First Ahitub heard a few sobs, then the entire crowd burst into mourning, wailing and sobbing and rending their garments. Some collapsed on the ground, weeping uncontrollably. Samuel had managed to bring their feelings to the surface, and now the emotions had nowhere else to go. It wasn't the kind of manipulation that Samuel had heard Hophni use when addressing the people, for he himself shared their grief and had to regain his own composure. For several minutes he stood head bowed in silence. Then, as the sounds of mourning died away, Samuel resumed speaking.

"They did not have the excuse of ignorance. More than a few among the dead had served at Shiloh. Although they knew of the sacredness of the ark, they still treated it as an object as common as the wagon that it had arrived in. Yet even if there had not been one Levite among the men of Beth-Shemesh, what happened there could have been avoided.

"It all comes back to the law, the same law that rested inside the ark, the law that we were commanded to teach to our children, to speak constantly of whatever we do. That law would have warned them that the ark was a holy thing and should have been treated as such.

"But there is no point in having a law and not obeying it, any more than in having seed and not planting it. I learned—I saw firsthand—that all the sacrifices ever offered at Shiloh were useless if there was no obedience to the law. For to obey is better than sacrifice, and to listen than the sacrifice of a fatted ram!"

Samuel stopped. Again the crowd seemed stunned for a few seconds. Then it surged forward and surrounded him, catching Ahitub in the crush. People swarmed around Samuel like bees. Few of them said anything, in some cases because they were too choked with emotion to speak. They wanted only to be close to him, to touch his garment or his hand or his hair. Ahitub had no idea what the people expected to happen. Some thrust things toward Samuel: clothing or food or articles of gold or silver. Although he would gently push the gifts away, Samuel never seemed to get angry at the people themselves. It felt like forever before enough people drifted away to allow Samuel to guide Ahitub away from the gate and back to their tent.

The boy watched his older brother as he started packing up the tent. Samuel appeared drained, worse than any day he'd come in from the fields to face the burden of his half brothers' scorn in addition to whatever work he'd had to do. What he'd just now said and done had taken almost everything out of him. They finished their work in silence and prepared to move on to the next city.

★   ★   ★

Gilgal lay east of Jericho, near the border that separated the tribe of Benjamin from that of Judah. The sun burned down as Samuel and Ahitub stood outside the city of Jerusalem before beginning their descent to Jericho and the Jordan Valley.

"We might want to stop and rest here," Samuel suggested. "It will take a long time to reach Jericho."

"How far down is it?"

"I don't know. But don't be surprised if you feel your ears pop."

The two of them ate and prepared to rest, only Ahitub wasn't tired. "What happened back there at Bethel?"

"What do you mean?"

"What you said to the people. You never sound like that at home."

"I know. But that's what I do when I travel as a judge. People ask for a message from the Lord, and if He gives me one, I pass it along."

Ahitub knew the intensity of Samuel's stories. He also realized that his older brother hadn't prepared beforehand what he was going to say, hadn't rehearsed anything. That, Samuel had told him, was the way of false seers such as Balaam. Ahitub could tell that he had built his story the way someone constructs a wall by carefully fitting stone on stone until the whole is solid and secure. And for his stones he was using what he had learned first from Hannah and then from Eli.

"Do you know what you're going to say before you say it?"

"Sometimes. I usually end up at the same place, no matter where I start."

"What place?"

"That obedience is better than sacrifice."

"That's important, huh?"

Samuel didn't answer at first. Ahitub was about to repeat the question when his brother said, "I learned just how important at Shiloh, when I was growing up there. When I was only a couple of years younger than you are now I realized that obedience is one of the most important things there is—and one of the hardest to achieve."

"How come?"

"The Lord gave us His law, and our happiness lies in obeying it. But for whatever reason it's not easy. I'd see the same people returning to Shiloh again and again, bringing sacrifices for the same sins. I didn't know why they couldn't just stop whatever it was they were doing. But I guess it gets too hard to quit after you've done something long enough."

"Like you and farming?"

"What?"

"Shemed and the others say you're not a very good farmer." As soon as he'd said it, Ahitub realized that perhaps it wasn't something that he should have mentioned.

"It's all right. I know I'm not very good at it. But I do seem to be good at this, so maybe it's just as well."

"Is it that hard to obey?" Ahitub asked, returning to their previous subject.

"It seemed to be especially hard for some of the Levites who lived and worked there. They performed the sacrifices and made the offerings, but it's as if they never learned anything from the rituals themselves."

"Do you ever want to go back there?"

"Part of me still does, although I know there's nothing there now."

"Can't the Lord start it up again?"

Samuel paused again, and when he spoke it was as if he was weighing each word carefully. "I suppose if He meant to He could. But He's said nothing about it."

"You think He will?"

"At the moment I think we have more important things to concern us. Now let's get some rest—it's going to be a long trek."

Ahitub laid down and prepared to sleep. He didn't really understand what Samuel had been talking about. Usually his words were a lot plainer and Ahitub could sort of tell what they meant, even if he didn't totally know for sure. Now, he told himself, his brother seemed to be only hinting at something. Maybe Samuel would say more later on. Right now, Ahitub was getting tired.

★   ★   ★

The descent from Jerusalem to Jericho was indeed a long one, taking almost until nightfall. Though the sun was warm, the highland air had an invigorating freshness about it as Samuel and Ahitub breathed it in before starting out. But soon enough, as they threaded their way down a barren wadi littered with boulders that they had to skirt, Ahitub could feel the air becoming heavier and damper, which only served to intensify the heat. Ahead he could see vast stretches of green as they approached the Jordan River valley. *Maybe it will feel better,* Ahitub thought, *when we get there.*

They plodded on, descending the 3,000 feet from Jerusalem until they arrived outside Jericho. Samuel decided to try to make his destination before the sun set.

"What's Gilgal like?" Ahitub asked, mainly as a way of taking his mind off the oppressive humidity.

"Well, it's not as big as Bethel, but it goes back a long way. It was one of the first places our ancestors lived after they'd crossed the river."

"If it's not as big, why come here?"

"Because it's within the lands of the tribe of Benjamin. I can't ignore it just because it's small."

"But it's so far away!"

"All the more reason to go. Sometimes people traveled great distances to go to Shiloh with their offerings—we certainly weren't going to turn them away."

"Did everybody come to Shiloh?"

"No," Samuel said as he shook his head. "Some people who, even though they lived nearby, never visited it, not even for the three feasts which everyone in Israel is supposed to attend."

"And that's why you're going to the people now, because they won't come to Ramah?"

"It's . . . not like that," Samuel smiled. "God hasn't commanded everyone to come to our house. I go here because . . . well, because people still need to hear about the law."

"If God starts up the tabernacle again, maybe it can travel from place to place too."

"That's not how it's supposed to be!" Now Samuel's voice was sharp, as if he'd lost the battle to control his temper. "God ordains that His people serve Him, not the other way around. Yes, it's hard for some people to get to Shiloh—some things *have* to be hard! How else will God know who is truly His?"

"I'm sorry, already!" Ahitub sulked.

"No," Samuel said in a quieter voice, "I'm sorry. It must be this heat." He glanced up at the sky, and only then realized that the sun was out of sight behind the hills to their back. It would be getting dark sooner than it had in Bethel. "Let's just keep moving." So they walked on in silence.

Approaching Gilgal just as the light was seriously starting to fade, they managed to build a quick fire and to pitch their tent before it was gone. They each ate a handful of food then fell asleep, exhausted by their travel.

Samuel arose early the next morning. He saw Ahitub still curled in slumber, breathing heavily, unaccustomed to the denser air. Getting up and stretching, Samuel left the tent and looked around. The sky was a dark blue, and everything else was just an indistinct shadow. It was far too early for anyone to be stirring. But Samuel was used to seeing the sky this color, from waking up at Shiloh to help Eli prepare for the morning sacrifice.

So many years ago, he thought, and still Shiloh continued to define his life.

He hadn't admitted it to himself, but Ahitub's questions about the sanctuary the day before had awakened a concern in him, one that he couldn't really address. Not now, anyway. Because he had one . . . no, *two* . . . stops to make after going to Mizpah and before returning to Ramah. One he *wanted* to make and the other he *had* to make. Samuel wondered whether Ahitub would understand, but decided in the end that he'd just have to bring the boy along and take the chance.

A rustling sound as Ahitub began to stir brought Samuel back to the tent.

They had pitched their tent in a small grove of Euphrates poplars within sight of Gilgal, so Samuel decided to leave everything where it was rather than set everything up all over again closer to the city. He told Ahitub, who immediately agreed, and the two of them started toward Gilgal.

Their pace had a certain laziness, borne of the humidity of the river valley to which neither of them were accustomed, just as there was a certain laziness in Samuel's decision to leave camp where it was. That, in fact, seemed to characterize the people of Gilgal when Ahitub watched them gather as word spread of Samuel's arrival. Perhaps it was from living in this humid valley where walking on a hot day felt more like swimming, where one couldn't see the great distances one could from the highland hills, and where water, because of the presence of the river, was something one took for granted rather than as a special blessing. Ahitub noticed less of a sense of urgency when the people of Gilgal had assembled.

The people were generally the kinds that he had seen at Bethel—farmers and craftspeople, the hawkers and the hopeful, the old and the curious. They looked pretty much the same, though their dress was somewhat fancier than that of the people in Bethel or even back in Ramah. Most had come to seek Samuel's counsel about things, but there seemed far fewer cases to hear than in Bethel. What cases there were had more to do with property damage and restoration than problems with boundaries. In half the cases flooding by the river had caused the damage, so the issue was how to bear the cost of restoration equitably. Even in the one case of a boundary dispute, the problem resulted from the uprooting of a particular tree by a flood. Samuel suggested the wording for a covenant between the two parties that would allow them to redefine the property.

As the morning wore on, the cases seemed to proceed with less urgency than Ahitub had seen at Bethel. It occurred to him that by leaving the highlands and descending into the Jordan Valley he had entered into a whole other country. Back home the mountainous terrain and poor soil had demanded that the people living there accustom themselves to hard work, and that seemed to make everybody as hard as a limestone outcropping. It certainly was the case with Peninah and her sons. They had an unyielding inflexibility about them in whatever they did, whether it was housekeeping or farming. Down here in the valley, though, lived people who never bothered to look up to the sky to wonder and worry whether it would rain, because there was no need. While Elkanah never was good at keeping his anxieties about each crop secret, Ahitub wondered to himself whether anyone living in the valley had to sell themselves into slavery the way he heard that some of their neighbors had to do after several crop failures in a row.

Ahitub then felt someone touching his shoulder, and woke from the half sleep of his thoughts. It was Samuel.

"Time to go back," he said.

The morning session had ended, and he'd heard only half of it! He was beginning to think that maybe this country magically put people to sleep. Getting up, he started to join Samuel.

But his brother had paused. Several men stood in front of Samuel, blocking his path. Two of them were strong, powerfully built, and didn't look at all friendly. Each carried a shepherd's rod in his belt, and one man rested his hand on it as if ready to draw it out.

The third man wore the finest clothes Ahitub had ever seen. Old, he had a beard that had gone almost white despite some gray spots. Yet Ahitub noticed his eyes most of all. Something about their cold and dark appearance frightened him. When the boy glanced at Samuel, he saw that his brother's face was hard as well—as if it had turned to stone.

"I heard that you were coming here," the old man said in a steady voice that seemed to belie his age. Samuel said nothing. "I remember when we last met. You were younger even than him," the stranger said as he nodded toward Ahitub in a way that made the boy shudder.

"I remember, Zeeb," Samuel told the wealthy landowner he had met so many years before.

"So you managed to outlive Eli and his sons. And Shiloh."

"I don't remember ever seeing you there."

The old man shrugged. "You can't remember what never happened. Or is that a seer's trick?"

"What do you want, Zeeb? My business is with the people of Gilgal."

"Let's just say I'm satisfying my curiosity. I hope Eli was pleased with the bullock you brought back to him."

"It wasn't a bullock," Samuel said, an undercurrent of anger in his voice. "It was a heifer, and you knew it when you had me get it."

"Still, I don't remember hearing any . . . complaints."

A faint smile touched Samuel's lips. "There was nothing to complain about—it turned out to be a red heifer."

Zeeb frowned. "Yes, I remember hearing that you priests burned it and used its ashes for . . . something or other," he said with a dismissive gesture. "How long has it been since Eli died?"

"As you well know, Eli's been dead for 10 years."

"Was it the Sea People?"

The man had asked the question in such a casual, careless manner that Ahitub feared that his brother was going to strike him. Instead, working hard to keep his anger in check, Samuel said, "He fell and broke his neck. It was the same day that the Sea People killed his sons."

"Pity," Zeeb said in a way that told Samuel that he really didn't care one way or the other. "Well, I really should rest now and suggest you do the same." Walking two paces toward Gilgal, he suddenly turned back.

"I have a place here in Gilgal, you know. So I'll be at the gate tomorrow to hear if the seer has any . . . messages . . . for me." With that he and the two men with him left.

Samuel spun on his heels and headed toward the grove where they had pitched their tent. Ahitub knew better than to try to talk to him. Something about Zeeb had made Samuel angry, and he didn't want to add fuel to the fire that raged inside his brother.

They ate little when they reached the tent, Samuel because he was too angry and Ahitub because the heat and humidity sapped his appetite. They said nothing to each other before laying down to sleep.

"Ahitub?"

The boy jerked awake. Still tired, he rubbed his eyes. "Do we have to go back to the gate?" he asked.

"Yes, it's time."

Stumbling to his feet, Ahitub left the tent. The sun was in a different place in the sky, but other than that it felt as if nothing had changed. It was as hot and stifling as ever. They started toward Gilgal.

"Ahitub, remember my telling you the story about the calf stuck in the mud?"

"I remember."

"It belonged to Zeeb, the old man who spoke to me before we returned to the tent."

"He must be old, huh?" Ahitub asked, easing his way into the topic by stating something obvious.

"Must be."

Silence. Ahitub thought it might be a good idea to change the subject. "Are we leaving tomorrow for Mizpah?"

"Yes."

"And then we're going home, right?"

"Not right away."

"Well, where are we going?"

But now they were close enough to the city gate that Samuel only replied, "We'll talk about that tonight."

Samuel spent the afternoon dealing with matters of the law. Again, as at Bethel, there seemed to be only a handful of people who asked about it in a way that gave Ahitub the impression that the answer would make a serious difference in their lives. He noticed two men, so alike they could have been twins, arguing between themselves as they approached the gate. They waited for a chance to address Samuel. When they did, only one of them said anything. He put a matter of law before Samuel to seek his answer. But when Samuel had answered them, the two turned around and seemed to pick up the argument where they had left it off, with one man saying that Samuel's words had proved his position and the other arguing that they did nothing of the kind.

The session ended not so much by any declaration as out of a sense that nothing more remained to discuss and nobody was interested enough to listen anyway. Samuel and Ahitub went back to their tent to prepare their evening meal.

"Nobody tried to give you anything," Ahitub commented halfway through their meal.

"You're right, they didn't." It was true. Not a single person from Gilgal had attempted to influence Samuel's decisions or pronouncements.

Ahitub thought about it. "Is that a good thing?" he asked.

"Not in this case."

"Why not?"

"It means that they don't care. They don't think it's important enough to try to buy my judgment."

"I'll bet Zeeb has all the money anyway." Then Ahitub gasped, afraid that his remark, made without thinking, would rekindle Samuel's anger.

Instead, Samuel sighed. "It wouldn't surprise me if he did."

"Doesn't he like you?"

"He probably hasn't thought twice about me since he almost sent me to my death all those years ago. It's easy to see what he loves: wealth and what you can do with it."

"Do you ever wish you had that kind of wealth?"

"Why do you ask?"

"I know Mother Peninah does."

"If being wealthy means getting it the way that Zeeb did," Samuel sighed, "then no, I don't. The Lord provides just enough, and that's fine with me."

"Oh. How do you know what's enough?"

"Well, too much wealth makes you forget God, and too little wealth makes you want to steal. Somewhere between them is . . . enough."

"Oh." Ahitub smiled. It looked as if Samuel wasn't going to get angry. They finished their meal in better spirits. Neither of them said it, but both of them were glad that they'd be departing in the morning.

★　★　★

Samuel and Ahitub both left their tent early for the city gate. The day promised to be hot again, and neither wanted to stay longer than necessary. Despite the oppressive heat a good number of people were waiting for Samuel. He quickly scanned the crowd, as if searching for someone. Ahitub guessed that he was looking for Zeeb. If Samuel saw the man, Ahitub couldn't tell from his expression. Then Samuel began speaking, and the murmur of conversation quickly ended.

"It was not far from here that our fathers first settled in this land. They crossed the river, a deed that in itself was miraculous. For Joshua did not arrogate to himself to be the first one to enter the land that the Lord had promised to the children of Jacob. No, it was the ark of the covenant, where the glory of the Lord dwelt, that was to lead them the last few steps out of slavery.

"So important was this, so sacred was the moment, that Joshua commanded the people to sanctify themselves the day before. So holy was this, that the Lord instructed Joshua to have the Levites carrying the ark to stop in the middle of the river. And when the Levites entered the river, its waters became as those of the Red Sea when they parted at the beginning of the journey of our ancestors from slavery in Egypt. As at the beginning, so it would be at the end.

"The ark stood in the middle of the river, a river that the Lord had caused not to flow until all had made it across. And while the people walked on a riverbed as dry as the southern desert, 12 men, one from each tribe, took one stone from the river and brought it up onto the western shore. Each stone was so big that they had to carry them on their shoulders.

"And why did the Lord command this?" Samuel paused, then glanced at Ahitub from the corner of his eye and smiled. "The Lord did this because He knew that children ask questions."

Ahitub watched the crowd. He didn't think that Samuel had lost any of his audience, but if he had been in any danger of doing so there was no threat of that now. People wanted to know where he was going with his speech.

"For Joshua declared," Samuel went on, "that one day the children of these people would ask their parents what those 12 stones meant. And they were to be told about how the Lord opened a way for our ancestors to escape slavery and to enter the land that He had prepared for them. For they were to say, 'The Lord our God dried up the waters of the Jordan before them until they had crossed over, as the Lord our God did to the Red Sea, which He dried up before them until they had crossed over, that all the peoples of the earth may know the hand of the Lord, that it is mighty, that you may fear the Lord your God forever.'

"God had those stones set up here—in Gilgal—to help us remember. But where are those who remember? Where are those who know the Lord and His holiness? Who are those who remember His law? It has become forgotten, and not just in Gilgal. The law—the first thing God gave to His people when they were finally beyond Pharaoh's reach—is one of the sacred objects that resides inside the ark of the covenant.

"But that ark fell into the hands of the Sea People. Not because they took it, but because the sons of Eli *gave* it to them. They who should have had the keenest knowledge of the ark committed the great sin of treating it as common!"

Ahitub remembered enough of Samuel's sermon at Bethel to know where he was going with his words.

"So the sons of Eli perished and the Sea People seized the ark. If you ask a hundred men what happened while the ark was in the possession of the Sea People you will get a hundred answers. For no one knows what truly happened . . . except the one to whom the Lord has revealed it."

Ahitub saw that the crowd, while still listening in a polite sort of way, didn't seem as attentive as those at Bethel. Samuel, however, continued as if it didn't matter.

"The Lord showed me the terrible vengeance He brought against the Sea People for their arrogance in thinking that they could make the Lord dance to their tune. It was an hubris at least as great as that of the sons of Eli. In each of the five great cities to which the Sea People took the Ark, cities that should belong to the children of Jacob, the people suffered the kind of plagues that befell Pharaoh when he refused to hear Moses. First mice overran the fields of the Sea People. Then the Sea People themselves suffered from painful boils. It became so bad that no city wanted anything to do with the ark, and they sent it away.

"And the Lord guided the ark on its return to His people. But what should have been a occasion of joy turned into a time of mourning. For I saw with my own eyes how many of our people fell dead in the fields of Beth-Shemesh. They perished because they were no different than the sons of Eli or the Sea People, each of whom treated the sacred ark and the law it contained as if it was something common. I saw our people lying out in the sun like flax drying on a roof. I saw the looks on their faces, the expressions of terror and fear.

"They were not in ignorance. More than a few among the dead had served at Shiloh. Even though they knew of the sacredness of the ark, they still treated it as something ordinary. Yet even if there had not been one Levite among the men of Beth-Shemesh, what happened there could have been avoided."

Ahitub was beginning to understand what Samuel was doing. At Bethel he had told the story of Jacob's dream as a way of bringing in the law, moving from it to the ark and from there to what had happened at Beth-Shemesh. Here at Gilgal he instead invoked the crossing of the Jordan to achieve the same end. He indeed was saying the same thing, yet differently. It was a skill that Ahitub couldn't fully understand, but also couldn't help admiring.

"It all comes back to the law," Samuel continued, "the same law that rested inside the ark, the law that God commanded us to teach to our children, to speak of when we lie down and when we rise up and when we walk by the way. That law would have warned them that the ark was a holy thing and should have been treated as such.

"But there is no point in having a law and not obeying it, any more than in having seed and not planting it. I learned—I saw firsthand—that all the sacrifices ever offered at Shiloh were useless if there was no obedience to the law. For to obey is better than sacrifice, and to listen than the sacrifice of a fatted ram!"

Samuel ended with the same words he had at Bethel. There, the outpouring of feeling when he concluded had been powerful as the people at the gate swarmed around him. Here at Gilgal, however, fewer of the people came forward to acknowledge him. Those who did had no less fervor than the inhabitants of Bethel, but others at the gate simply resumed talking to each other or else walked away to do something else. Ahitub even recognized the two brothers still arguing with each other. Perhaps they still hadn't resolved their discussion from last time.

When Samuel had finished speaking with the last of the people who approached him, he noticed one man watching him through narrowed eyes. The person approached Samuel, and Ahitub recognized him as one of the men who had been standing behind Zeeb the day before. When Samuel saw who it was, his expression hardened.

"Is Zeeb here?" he asked.

"Zeeb is dead," the man said as casually as if he were saying "The sky is blue."

"What?"

"He died in his sleep last night and will be buried before the day is over."

"You speak very coldly of your master."

"Zeeb was my father."

If the announcement of Zeeb's death had startled Samuel, he was shocked now. This man was a son of Zeeb? This man whose face was like granite, whose clothes weren't rent in mourning, whose eyes were as dry as midsummer ground? His father was dead, and yet he just stood there?

"What do you want?" Samuel asked finally.

"I was just wondering whether you might stay in Gilgal."

"Why, do you want me to remain?"

"Frankly, I don't. But somebody should help settle our father's inheritance. He bred sons as if they were cattle and never told any of us what was to become of his wealth when he died."

"Why ask me? Can't you work this out yourselves?"

"You don't know what you're asking," the man said in a flat voice. "None of us trusts the other to do justly. Because you're a stranger, that's something in your favor. If you do well, you can probably claim a share for yourself."

"No," Samuel said almost instantly. "I won't be judge over another man's house. You'll have to work this out among yourselves." With that, he strode back to their tent, Ahitub hurrying close behind. They broke camp in silence, tied their provisions on their donkey, then started the climb up out of the Jordan Valley and back to the highlands and on to Mizpah. It was an exhausting journey, and the two had to stop several times and rest. Physically and emotionally, the two of them didn't start to feel like their old selves until they were close to the city of Jerusalem. It was only then that Ahitub said what he'd been thinking ever since leaving the gate at Gilgal.

"I'll bet Zeeb died just to spite you!"

★　★　★

When the Lord promised the land of Canaan to the sons of Jacob he had appointed six cities of refuge. They were places to which persons accused of committing a crime and who claimed that they were innocent could then flee. There they would be safe from those seeking blood vengeance until their case could receive a hearing.

That was the theory, anyway. In practice, any city that declared itself a haven for those accused of wrongdoing tended to attract those who lived by rough rules. Mizpah was one of those cities, a city of refuge that had been the home of Jephthah, one of the *shoftim.* Samuel knew all this, which was why he felt as if a rock had lodged in his stomach as the city came into view. It would have been easy enough to have traveled in a circle to Mizpah, then Bethel, then Gilgal, and finally home to Ramah. Instead, Samuel made Mizpah the last stop on his route.

Ahitub, on the contrary, was excited when he first saw the place. After Gilgal, he was glad to be back in the central highlands. Like Samuel, he felt that he could breathe once more. As warm as it was in the highlands during the months of vine tending, the Jordan Valley's oppressive humidity had been worse. Still, he didn't know anything of Mizpah's reputation and Samuel worried that he might find it even more exciting if he did. So he had said nothing about its reputation.

They arrived late in the afternoon, having slept longer than usual through midday to recover from the trip up from Jericho to Jerusalem. After making camp within sight of the city walls, they ate frugally of their diminishing store of food and fell asleep.

A few hours later, however, Samuel awakened and decided to stay up for a while, keeping watch. The fire had died, but the cloudless, moonless sky was full of stars and there was no need for light. Samuel surveyed the land around him, everything bathed in the ice-blue radiance of the stars.

Good, Samuel thought. This way he could still see if anything—or anyone—approached them. Between what he had heard at Shiloh and what he had learned since returning to Ramah and helping to tend his father's flocks, he had a good awareness of the dangerous animals that roamed the highlands at night: the lion and the wolf, the hyena and the bear. But he wasn't as concerned about their threat so much as he was about who might have watched them from the city walls while they pitched their tent. After about an hour with no sign of anything, his exhaustion overwhelmed his apprehension and he went back to sleep inside the tent.

Morning came eventually, and Samuel slowly sat up. Not having slept well, he shook his head as if to clear the weariness from it. It didn't help. Jostling Ahitub's shoulder to awaken him, he then got to his feet and started to leave the tent.

Halfway out, he stopped. Someone sat in front of the tent, not five paces from him. The man was a little older than Samuel himself, was as solidly built as a large storage jar, and his midnight-black hair and beard seemed to defy any attempt at control. He looked at Samuel, who couldn't help swallowing.

"Are you the judge who comes here?"

"I am."

Rising to his feet, the man put his hands on his belt. Samuel then noticed the bronze dagger tucked into it.

"My brother's been accused of killing someone."

Samuel waited for him to add something along the lines of "I want you to declare him innocent . . . or else!" But the man just silently stared at Samuel.

"If he wants me to hear his case," Samuel said, measuring his words carefully, "I will."

The man still didn't say anything in response but merely nodded, turned, and walked back toward Mizpah.

Trembling slightly, Samuel remained where he was. He was convinced that he had just received a death threat if his ruling wasn't to the man's liking.

Seconds later Ahitub stepped out of the tent, stretching. "Who was that?" he asked.

"Someone who wanted to talk to me about a decision I may have to make."

"What did he offer?" the boy asked, remembering the way the people of Bethel had sought to buy Samuel's favor.

"Something as precious as my own life."

"What?" Ahitub said, intrigued.

"I—I was just joking," Samuel replied, trying to sound casual. "Let's get ready—we'll be leaving soon."

Before long Samuel and Ahitub neared the gate of Mizpah. Of the three cities they had been to, Ahitub considered Mizpah to be the most impressive. The walls surrounding it were enormous despite the fact that Samuel had told him the city was not very large. As they got closer, he could see that they rested on enormous boulders. The walls, like the land that surrounded them, were of limestone. The rectangular towers that rose above and out of the wall in several places especially fascinated Ahitub.

As with the other two cities, a crowd had gathered at the gate. Ahitub recognized the same kinds of people: vendors and laborers and those with nothing else to do. But he also noticed that the people here did not exhibit the sense of welcome that he had received as a stranger even at Gilgal. The people of Mizpah, it seemed, were sullen, silent, suspicious. Even the business of hawking and buying goods a short distance away from where Samuel had seated himself went on as if under a cloud. A shift of the eyes seemed to convey as much as a broad gesture to these people. It scared him to see it, though he wasn't sure why it should.

Soon Samuel began hearing cases. The first was mercifully routine. One man had accused another of stealing food. The thief pleaded hunger as the reason. When asked if he could restore what he had taken, the thief admitted that he had nothing, that he had lost his livelihood with the sale of his former master's farm. Samuel managed to negotiate a certain amount of restitution that the thief would pay after he succeeded in finding work at the gate. Both sides only grudgingly accepted the settlement, but it was still at least an agreement.

Then Samuel heard a case unlike any of the others he had encountered so far. Most until then had involved crimes of property— theft or attempted theft. Now a man named Daah began by announcing in a matter-of-fact manner, "They say I murdered someone: Omri son of Caleb."

"Did you murder him?" Samuel questioned.

"No. I just killed him, that's all."

"Why did you kill him?"

"My sister was gleaning in a field outside of the city. He raped her. I heard about it, so I killed him. I really don't see what the problem is here. The law of Moses says I have the right!"

"So it does," Samuel answered softly. Not for the first time, it struck him that the people of Mizpah had a greater knowledge of the law of Moses than the inhabitants of Bethel or Gilgal. Or at least a more extensive awareness of certain provisions.

"I mean, it's not as if it happened within the city!"

"Where did this happen?"

"As I said, in a field outside of the city."

"Whose field?"

"His name's Caleb, son of Ahaz."

When Samuel glanced at the crowd, his heart jumped as he saw the man with the black hair lurking toward the rear. Finding his voice, he asked, "Were there any witnesses?"

Daah's anger flared a little. "What witnesses? They were in the field of Caleb!"

"And is the woman here?"

"No, she was too ashamed. She won't leave her house."

"And she told you what had happened?"

More anger flashed across Daah's face. "Of course she did!"

"Then why can't she tell me herself?"

A long uncomfortable silence. Folding his arms in front of him, Daah glared at Samuel, but said nothing.

"Unless she is brought to the gate," Samuel continued, "there is no way to determine the truth of what you have to say. And I would be forced to conclude that you had no cause to kill Omri."

Daah jerked his head and unfolded his arms. "Very well, I'll go get her!"

"*We* will go get her," Samuel said as he got to his feet. "I and two of the elders of Mizpah will accompany you."

Ahitub saw the man's hands clench into fists. Samuel knew the risk he was taking, but he had to make sure that the two of them couldn't rehearse a story on their way back to the gate.

"Fine!" Daah said in disgust, then walked back into the city accompanied by Samuel and two old men whom, to their surprise, Samuel had enlisted as escorts.

"Ahitub," he said after a moment's hesitation, "you come too but stay close."

Following Daah, they entered the city. As with any other city, it appeared to have sprung up haphazardly. It always reminded Samuel of his first time in Jericho, when he had accompanied Abdon to retrieve what was supposed to be a bullock from Zeeb. Mizpah was no better laid out than Jericho, he thought. Once again he found himself missing the order of the sanctuary encampment.

Samuel and Ahitub followed Daah closely. Twice they had to ask him not to go so fast, to allow the elderly men from the gate to catch up. When they had to request it a third time, however, he ignored them.

"I said slow down!"

Suddenly Daah darted straight ahead down the narrow street, shouldering several people out of his way before dodging to his right and disappearing down a side street.

"He's running away!" Ahitub shouted, then started running after him. Almost immediately Samuel grabbed the boy by the back of his cloak and held him fast.

"No!" Samuel ordered.

"But we don't know where he's going!"

"We also don't know whether he isn't waiting around that corner with a knife in his hand!"

"Oh."

Ahitub hadn't thought of that, and now that Samuel had brought up the possibility he felt his legs start to shake. He reached out and took hold of Samuel's hand, squeezing it tight.

"So," one of the escorts wheezed to Samuel, "now we should go back."

"Back?"

"Back to the gate. He's not going anywhere." With that, the two old men began to slowly retrace their steps.

"What did you mean he's not going anywhere?" Samuel asked when he and Ahitub had caught up with them.

"Daah won't leave Mizpah, no matter how well he hides. He's safer here than out in the open," one of the men said.

"And that doesn't bother you?"

"Not as long as we know where he is."

Samuel had heard several capital cases, most of them here in Mizpah, but never one that had taken this particular turn. "But what about Omri?"

"If the talk at the gate is to be believed," the other elderly man said, "Omri probably didn't rape his sister."

"Then what happened?"

"From what we've heard, the sister was giving herself to men in the service of the gods of the Canaanites, letting them lie with her at the high places around here."

Samuel glanced at Ahitub, who was still looking nervously over his shoulder to see if Daah was following them. It was clear the boy wasn't paying attention to what the old men were saying, or else if he was, he didn't understand what they were talking about.

"And you believe it?"

"It sounds about right."

"He probably became suspicious, so she made up the rape story," the other man suggested. "She probably didn't mean to single out Omri."

"Might have been the first name that came to her head when her brother questioned her," the first man wheezed.

"But without the word of the sister—" Samuel began.

"Without the word of his sister Daah is trapped here," the second man interrupted. "Omri's kinsmen will be watching the gate for any sign of him, and you know they'll kill him if he ever shows his face. One way or another he'll die here in Mizpah. Probably when he's as old as we are."

"Pity. It's been a while since we had a good stoning," the first man sighed.

"What about that couple caught in adultery last month?" his companion said.

"Oh, yes, now I remember . . ."

The two men rambled on about the rough justice of Mizpah in a way that reminded Samuel of listening to Elkanah discussing rain and cattle with another of the local farmers. It was all so casual, so easy! He glanced once more at Ahitub to see whether the conversation was upsetting him. Fortunately, Ahitub was still too frightened to pay any attention, and he didn't let go of Samuel's hand until they had found their way back to the city gate.

Pulling himself together, Samuel declared to the assembled people that Daah was a fugitive who should be apprehended if seen, brought to the city gate, and stoned to death. Those at the gate nodded in assent, either simply because it made sense or perhaps because it gave them something to look forward to.

Samuel then asked if anyone else had another case, but nobody said anything. When Samuel scanned the crowd at the gate once more, he realized that the man with the black hair had disappeared. Had he followed them into the city? Was he possibly waiting around the corner to prevent Samuel from capturing the murderer?

Glancing at the sky, Samuel felt that it was close enough to midday to suspend the proceedings. He and Ahitub returned to their tent, even more grateful to be away from Mizpah as they had been to leave the Jordan Valley.

They ate their first meal of the day in silence, and it was only when the two of them were preparing to sleep that Ahitub asked, "Do we have to go back there?" His voice had an unmistakable quaver to it.

"Yes, we do. We should at least find out if there are any points of the law that they need to hear."

"Oh." Ahitub was clearly not enthusiastic about the prospect.

"Don't worry," Samuel said as reassuringly as possible, "I won't let anything happen to you."

His assurance, as hollow as it sounded to Samuel, seemed to calm Ahitub's fears, and soon they both were asleep. In fact, both of them slept soundly and woke up refreshed. They returned to Mizpah in a considerably lighter mood than when they had left it a few hours before.

As they approached the gate they noticed a crowd of people milling outside it. Whatever they were doing, it was kicking up a good amount of dust. Realizing that something had happened, Samuel told Ahitub to wait for him, then walked toward the group.

As he came closer, he saw that many of the people in the group held bundles of twigs in their hands and were waving them over the ground in sweeping motions. But he saw nothing on the limestone flat except a number of good-sized rocks . . .

Then it hit Samuel. He recognized what the people were doing. They weren't sweeping dust away; they were brushing it onto one specific spot in order to absorb something.

Blood. Growing up at the sanctuary had taught Samuel to recognize instantly what blood mingling in the dust looked like. He had watched the priests and novices sweeping it away after every major sacrifice and its attendant slaughter.

Someone in the crowd kicked aside one of the stones and it rolled to a stop at Samuel's feet. It was about as big around as his fist—and it had a dark stain on it.

"You missed it."

Startled, Samuel looked up to see the man with the dagger. He stared with cold eyes as dark as midnight, eyes that betrayed nothing.

"You missed it," the man repeated. "My brother was caught, brought to the gate, and, as you ordered, stoned for having committed murder."

"Where . . . ?" Samuel began.

"Buried. We're not supposed to leave a dead body in the open. That's in the law of Moses, right?"

Samuel nodded. He tried to keep his attention on the man's eyes, but found himself glancing at the knife he still wore in his belt.

"Don't worry," the man said, his face and voice still expressionless. "Justice was done. That's what really matters, right?" Then, without waiting for an answer, he vanished into the city. As he walked away, the two old men who had accompanied Samuel approached him.

"You missed it. Too bad—it was very well done," one of them said to Samuel.

"But it wasn't as if we could wait until after midday, was it?" the other added.

"Who brought him to the gate?" Samuel asked.

"Didn't you know? Of course not; you weren't here. His own brother."

"His brother?"

"You were just talking to him a minute ago."

"It was done right, like I said. Threw the first stone himself."

"But—but his own brother! Did they hate each other that much?"

"Hate had nothing to do with it. We weren't sure whether or not Daah was guilty. When he ran, that pretty much decided it."

"His brother came to my tent this morning," Samuel said, somewhat dazed about what had happened. "I had thought he'd come to plead for Daah's life."

"And he probably would have, too, if he had thought Daah was innocent. Nobody knew for certain. But now we do. Guess the Lord worked everything out."

"After all," the other old man said, "brothers don't tell each other everything, right?"

"Right," Samuel said weakly. He glanced over at the place where the stoning had taken place. The people of Mizpah had erased all traces of justice. Numbly Samuel took his seat at the gate.

The afternoon session was a blur. He spent it answering questions about the law. As he suspected, most of them centered on only a few points, questions honed so fine they were as sharp and narrow as a needle. Yet no matter how complex the question, Samuel phrased his answers in such a way that he left his hearers no room to think they could make the law say whatever they wanted it to. Nobody argued with his pronouncements and some even seemed to grant him a grudging respect. But when Samuel took Ahitub back with him to their tent, he was as emotionally spent as he had been physically exhausted by the climb up to Jerusalem.

"I don't think I understood what you said," Ahitub admitted over their food.

"I'm not surprised. They weren't ordinary questions about the law."

"Well, why did they ask what they did?"

"To find ways to get around the law and do what they want to do," he said with a sigh.

That seemed to satisfy Ahitub for a few moments; then he blurted, "What's the law for, anyway?"

Samuel smiled, something he hadn't done much of that day. "I remember asking Eli something like that. He'd said that the law tells us what sins we are to avoid, and I asked him, 'But what's *sin?*' I don't think he was quite ready for that one."

"What *is* it?"

"As I came to learn it, it has to do with how we are toward God, whether we want to follow the Lord or just go our own way. When we go our own way, we walk away from Him and His people. That's sin. Understand?"

"I think so," the boy said slowly.

"The law's much more than a list of things that we aren't supposed to do, as important as that might be. It's also about what we can and should do in our lives."

"Like all the stuff about gleaning?"

"Exactly! We let poor people and strangers glean at the edges of our fields because we were once poor and strangers when we were in Egypt. Not us personally," Samuel hastened to add, "but when our ancestors lived there and brought us out of Egypt. God showed kindness to us, so we ought to display the exact same kindness to one another."

"What about what happened to the man?"

"That's . . . something different," Samuel said, a sadness in his voice. "That's what happens when sin is at its worst. Someone could be standing right in front of you—as close as you and I are to each other—but because that person's heart has walked so far away from God, they can never come back."

"How do you know when that happens?"

"By what they do: by stealing or killing or . . . doing other things."

"What other things?"

"We'll save that for another time. It's getting late, and we have a long way to travel tomorrow."

"Where are we going?"

"Let's just say it's someplace I know very well," he said with a light in his eyes. "It's times to sleep now."

"All right. What will you say to the people tomorrow?"

"I don't know for certain."

"You're going to end by telling them that obeying is better than sacrificing, though, right?"

"You *have* been listening!"

"But where are you going to start?"

"We'll see."

★   ★   ★

Ordinarily Samuel would have put off packing his tent and provisions until after he had said his farewell to the people of a city. The
following morning, however, he would have liked nothing better
than to pack everything and have it ready to go, so that he wouldn't
have to stay any longer than necessary. He knew, however, that it
would be a supremely insulting gesture, so he and Ahitub left things
as they were and returned once more to the gate at Mizpah.

The crowd had gathered as usual. One thing Samuel couldn't
help sensing, though: they were more expectant as to what he had
to say than the people at Gilgal had been. Perhaps that's why he
found the city so disconcerting. While the people might have been
interested in the law in order to shape it to their own ends, they
were interested all the same. He stood before the people now, prepared to speak.

But he still didn't know what to say. His mind had gone blank.

Nobody in the crowd seemed impatient, but a few clearly picked
up on his prolonged silence. Breathing a quick prayer for help, he
looked over the crowd. At the far end on his right stood Daah's
brother, his arms folded before him, that bronze knife flashing in the
sunlight, flashing red like . . .

With a quick and silent prayer of thanksgiving, Samuel began.

"Blood. We cannot avoid it. We are all born in blood. When
the navel string is cut there is blood. When a male is circumcised on
the eighth day there is blood. And when justice is required, as it was
here yesterday, there is blood.

"You people of Mizpah know that as well as anyone—maybe
more so. You live in one of the cities of refuge established in this
land. The Lord had a purpose for such cities. They weren't meant to
be cracks in a mountain where someone could hide to escape God's
presence. Our great seer Moses hid himself in such a crack only because he asked to see the one thing that no one can look upon and
live: the unshielded glory of the Lord.

"Yet some would think that the cities of refuge are themselves
places of blood. They assume such cities attract those who shed blood.

"This was never the Lord's intent. He established the cities of refuge not to enable us to shed blood, but to prevent the shedding of blood—the blood of the innocent.

"I have seen the shedding of the blood of the innocent. It was almost the first thing I saw in the morning and almost the last thing I saw at sunset. The cities of refuge cannot compare with the sanctuary of the Lord as a place for the shedding of blood.

"And though it has been gone 10 years now, I remember it as if it were yesterday. Every morning the high priest Eli would spill the blood of a lamb, an innocent creature that had harmed no one. Its life would be taken, and it would be consumed whole on the altar of sacrifice. Then Eli would enter the tabernacle. Going into the holy place, he would mingle some of the blood of that lamb with the incense that burned in the presence of the Lord. Morning and evening this happened, and I watched it every day for eight years."

Ahitub glanced at the crowd. He could see several people nodding thoughtfully, almost approvingly.

"Why was so much blood shed? It wasn't spilled in anger, as the blood of Abel had been when Cain murdered him. There was no sense of anger or retribution about what happened. It was precisely because the lamb had done nothing, *because* of the lamb's innocence, that it had been slain.

"And why was it slain? Because God ordained it in His holy law. He stipulated that sin must be answered by death. But because He could not bear that any of us who were created in His image should die, He accepted in place of our death the death of something innocent, something as sinless as the Lord Himself. The lambs that I have spoken of—they were sacrificed for you, and for you, and for you, and for all Israel!"

Ahitub heard a muffled sound coming from somewhere in the crowd. Was someone crying?

"For the law of God requires that sin must be answered by death. And rather than destroy all who dwell upon the earth, He has given us His law, that we might learn it, and heed it, and avoid death at His hands.

"Yesterday you saw one struck dead outside the city gate. Some of you may have participated in that death, while others merely assented to it. But I've also seen death, and not just the deaths of ani-

mals, of sheep and goats and oxen. I once looked upon 70 men—
70—all struck dead in one day!

"The Lord showed me the terrible vengeance He brought
against the Sea People for their arrogance in thinking that the Lord
and His law meant nothing. In each of the five great cities to which
the Sea People took the ark of the covenant, cities that should belong to the children of Jacob, the people suffered the kind of plagues
that befell the people of Egypt when Pharaoh refused to hear Moses.
It became so bad that no city wanted anything to do with the ark,
and they sent it away.

"And the Lord guided the ark on its return to His people. But
what should have been a occasion of joy turned into a time of mourning. For I saw with my own eyes where 70 of our people fell dead in
the fields of Beth-Shemesh. They perished because they treated the sacred ark and the law it contained as if it were something common. I
saw where they lay out in the sun like flax drying on a rooftop. I saw
the looks on their faces, the expressions of terror and fear.

"What made their sin of disrespect for the ark worthy not only
of condemnation but of death was the fact that they had been at the
tabernacle. They had been Levites, serving there when I was there.
Each of them knew that the ark and the law that it contained were
sacred, and yet they did nothing about it. Their deaths are all the
sadder because they need not have happened!

"Yet even if there had not been one Levite among the men of
Beth-Shemesh, what happened there could have been avoided. It all
comes back to the law, the same law that rested inside the ark, the
law that God commanded us to teach to our children, to speak of
when we lie down and when we rise up and when we walk by the
way. That law would have warned them that the ark was a holy
thing and should have been treated as such.

"But there is no point in having a law and not obeying it, any
more than in having seed and not planting it. Had they observed
and obeyed the law, they would not have died. Had the one who
was stoned outside this gate yesterday known and heeded the law
of the Lord, his blood would not have had to be shed. I learned—
I saw firsthand—that all the sacrifices ever offered at Shiloh were
useless if there was no obedience to the law. For to obey is better

than sacrifice, and to listen than the sacrifice of a fatted ram!"

As Samuel finished speaking, Ahitub once again felt admiration for him. But concern quickly replaced the feeling, since he wasn't sure how the people of Mizpah would react. After the events of the past few days he didn't know what to expect.

But as at Bethel, the people of Mizpah who had come to hear Samuel surged forward and expressed their appreciation. They seemed to mean it, too. A few tried pressing gifts upon him, but Samuel as usual refused them all.

One of those who approached him was the brother of Daah. As Ahitub saw him withdraw the bronze knife from his belt, the boy's heart stopped. There were too many people between him and Samuel to get to it, and it appeared as if he wouldn't have any time to warn his brother. But no sooner had Ahitub realized what was happening than he saw the man try to press the handle of the knife into Samuel's hand. But the seer declined this gift as he had done all the others, though with somewhat more tact. Still, he was close enough to hear the man say, in a flat and unemotional tone, "Fine, I'll keep it then. But if you ever need it, send word."

"I . . . will," Samuel said, unsure of what the man meant by that. After accepting the thanks of a few more people, Samuel and Ahitub returned to their tent. Ahitub glanced over his shoulder at the spot where Daah had been stoned the day before. It looked perfectly ordinary.

★　★　★

It was a hard ride north to Lebonah, though not because it was difficult terrain. They were still in the highlands and what might have been rough traveling to someone from the Jordan Valley or from the coastal plains was second nature to Samuel and Ahitub. What concerned them was time. The two of them had left Mizpah on Preparation Day, and Samuel was eager to arrive at Lebonah and set up their camp before sunset. He wanted the coming Sabbath to be special.

Sabbaths at the home of Elkanah weren't like those at the sanctuary. With so many people to feed and so many animals to tend, it was hard for Samuel to detect the kind of Sabbath rhythm he had felt as Eli's helper. True, Hannah worked harder to prepare food on Preparation Day than she did during the rest of the week, but it seemed as if she never cooked enough. What's more, the sons of Peninah didn't seem to take the Sabbath seriously. Although Shemed treated his own rest seriously enough, he didn't hesitate to order the others about if some of the animals needed tending. As for Izhar, Samuel had come to learn that he didn't take a lot of things seriously. And even during those Sabbaths when the family was together they were still divided in heart, with the sons of Peninah avoiding the sons of Hannah. Lebiya traded insults with her brothers as freely then as on any other day.

So it was with a glad heart that Samuel caught sight of Lebonah in the distance as the sun hovered close to the western horizon. Finding a spot to pitch their tent near a crossroad south of the city, Samuel and Ahitub started cooking their evening meal as the sun touched the horizon.

"Is this all we have left?" Ahitub asked as he looked into the cooking pot.

"Almost."

"Why couldn't we have gone home?"

"I told you, we still have two more places to go."

"Which two places?"

"You'll see."

No matter how hard Ahitub peppered Samuel with questions, he couldn't learn their destination. He gave up about the time the evening stew was ready. Ahitub was afraid it would be thin, but it turned out to be quite flavorful. He finished sopping up the remains with his bread and looked up as the stars emerged in the cloudless summer sky. Unable to resist, he stepped away from the fire, lay down on his back, and watched the sky darken and the heavens light up. Samuel joined him as they silently observed the Lord make His eternal presence known by the gradual unfolding of His creation. When he had nodded off for the second time, Samuel suggested that maybe they'd better go inside the tent and get some sleep. As they did, Ahitub wondered why every Sabbath couldn't be like this.

The boy awoke the next morning assuming that he and Samuel

would spend the day there. Instead, Samuel announced that they would head west.

"What's there?" the boy asked.

"You'll see."

They started down the road that led up a long valley. Samuel's pace slowed noticeably at a certain point. Ahitub didn't see any-thing unusual—just a valley covered with grass, shrubs, and a few thickets. Samuel, however, had stopped and was scanning every inch of the terrain.

"Where are we?" Ahitub finally asked.

"Home."

"Home?"

"I'll show you," he said as he led their donkey along. Soon he stopped, helped Ahitub dismount, and looked around him once more.

"This is where I grew up," Samuel said after a minute of search-ing, a touch of melancholy in his voice, melancholy mixed with fondness. "This is where the sanctuary once stood."

Ahitub scanned the valley. "Where?"

"I'll show you," Samuel said as he pulled a short goad from the things packed on the donkey's back. He walked to a spot, checked himself, glanced around again, then started using the goad to draw a line on the ground. Ahitub went over to see.

"What are you doing?"

"I'm showing you where the curtain around the sanctuary used to be. You see these small dimples in the ground? They used to hold the silver sockets."

"Every one?"

"Yes, and there were a lot of them. Poles sat in each of them, and linen curtains hung from the poles. Now here," he said, point-ing to a flat area of grass and limestone, "was where the altar of sac-rifice stood. This," he said as he indicated a slight rise in the ground, "used to be a ramp that led up to it. It's been worn down—it once was higher."

"How high?"

"About as tall as you."

"Really?"

"Really. The fire in the altar burned all the time. We used to put the ashes from the fire and some of the animal parts from the sacrifices over in this corner. One of the novices would later take it all to the trash heap outside the compound. Let's see, the laver used to be about here. That's where the priests washed their hands and feet . . ."

Samuel's words trailed off as he saw the expression on Ahitub's face. The boy had kept a respectful silence, but it was clear that his brother was seeing a world that Ahitub couldn't even begin to imagine. The fire that had begun to spring up in his heart died down a little.

"I'm sorry—I must sound pretty foolish."

"No, no, I . . . I just wish I could have seen it."

"I wish you . . . never mind. I just want to look at one more thing." He walked west and stopped at a patch of grass. Kneeling down, he placed a hand on it. Ahitub walked over to him. "What's that?" he asked.

"This spot is where the ark of the covenant once stood," he said quietly. "And it was here that we helped bury the high priest Eli when he died."

"Oh."

Samuel rose from where he had been kneeling. "Remember this place, Ahitub."

"All right. What now?"

"Now, there's someone I want you to meet."

Samuel guided the donkey north up a short side valley that led off the main one. At the end of the valley huddled a small village. Samuel confidently walked through it to a small house. Ahitub sniffed the air. "What is that?"

"That's clay," Samuel said as he knocked on the door of the house.

"If you're here on business, go away!" a gruff voice called out from inside. "This is the Sabbath."

"I know, Issachar!" Samuel called out.

Ahitub heard a rustling inside and the door opened a moment later. An old man stood before him, leaning his hand on the door-way. He stuck the other hand out in front of him, and only then did Ahitub realize that the man Samuel called Issachar was blind. As he watched Issachar and Samuel embrace, he remembered all the stories that his brother had told him about the blind, garrulous Levite whom everybody else ignored or else treated with contempt, but who had eventually become a potter for the sanctuary compound.

Seeing him now was an odd sensation for Ahitub. Issachar had come to have a strange sort of reality in his mind. The boy knew that there was such a person, but he existed in the same way that Moses or Adam or anyone else in the stories that Samuel told him existed. Although he realized that there was such a person, he had never thought that he would ever see someone from Samuel's past. Until now.

"So what are you doing here?" Issachar asked. "I'm guessing you haven't run out of questions."

"Nothing like that. I brought someone to met you. Ahitub, this is Issachar the potter."

"Hello," the boy said shyly.

"That's not going to help me," Issachar said, the old sharpness in his voice. "You'll have to step closer."

Ahitub did so, and as a result had to endure the blind potter's hands examining him from the top of his head to his shoulders, down his arms, and across his chest.

"Yes, I can see the resemblance," Issachar said. Puzzled, Ahitub didn't notice Samuel's face turning red. "So what *does* bring you here?"

"We've been out," Ahitub volunteered. "Samuel's been judging."

"That time of year, is it? Shouldn't be surprised. It's about this time that people start ordering jugs for wine. The harvest of the summer fruit will be soon."

"Does Samuel always come to see you?"

"Yes, he always drops by to see me. Of course, I can never see him! I'm sorry, but I don't have very much to prepare for a Sabbath meal."

"That's all right, Issachar," Samuel replied. "I'm sure we can make something satisfying between what you have and what we brought with us."

"Then we'd better get started. Food won't get prepared by talking to it."

"Go on, Ahitub," Samuel said. With that, the boy walked to the donkey and started foraging through their stores. As he did so, Issachar reached out, took hold of Samuel's sleeve, pulling him close.

"The boy doesn't know, does he?"

"No, Issachar," Samuel said in an awkward whisper, "he doesn't."

"Are you planning on telling him sometime?"

"Yes, but . . . it's so hard to know when would be the best."

"Seems as if there's never a good or convenient time to tell the truth. You should know that as well as anyone. But don't worry; I won't say anything while you two are here. I wouldn't dream of robbing you of that honor."

Samuel was too embarrassed to say anything. Fortunately, Ahitub approached them with their food. In a short time the talk within the small and disorderly house turned to Samuel's circuit of judging and of prophesying, then to the days when the sanctuary still stood and how a small boy had come to befriend a blind Levite.

"You two were friends, weren't you?" Ahitub asked.

"If we were," Issachar replied, "we were an odd pair of friends. I think we were more curious about each other than anything else." Issachar paused and ran one hand through his hair. "That's all gone now, and the Sea People didn't have to raise a finger. We did it to ourselves," he added bitterly.

"Are you worried about the Sea People?"

"The boy's picked up your habit of asking senseless questions, Samuel. No, I'm not worried about them, boy. I'm old enough now that death doesn't worry me, however it comes."

Ahitub blushed, afraid he'd said the wrong thing.

"He does have a point," Samuel said. "What if they decide to push inland?"

"But it doesn't make sense, boy! They've seized the coastal plains, and I don't think they're used to living and fighting here in the hill country. What would they gain from charging up here and fighting us, tell me that!"

"Land?" Ahitub said almost as a reflex.

Issachar opened his mouth to say something, paused with it still open, then chuckled. "Yes, I suppose there's that," the old potter finally decided. "If they've come all this way to capture a place, I don't suppose they'll stop with what's convenient. They might as well try to take it all."

"Have there been any attacks yet?" Samuel questioned.

"Not that I've heard. I know they're still west of here in Aphek, down on the plain. But they'd have to come through Lebonah to get here, and we've had no reports of their trying to take it. Or of their doing business with it, for that matter."

"Business?" Samuel echoed in surprise.

Issachar put his hand to his mouth, as if to take back the words he had just spoken. Something about the silence unnerved Ahitub. Then Issachar leaned toward Samuel. "Is the door closed?" he whispered.

"Yes."

Without a word, the blind man rose, then felt his way to a line of jugs in one corner of the house. Reaching in, he withdrew something and handed it to Samuel.

It was a dagger, but not like any that Samuel had seen before. The blade had something odd about it. At first he thought it was silver, but it looked too different, too dull, to be silver.

"Feel the blade on that," Issachar quietly urged. It had a sharp, straight blade.

"Now try to bend it." Samuel did, but try as he might, it resisted his efforts.

"What is it?" Samuel asked as he handed it back and Issachar replaced it in the jug.

"That, boy," the potter said as he sat back down, "is a piece of something that hasn't been seen since close to the Creation. You know all the stories, so you'd recognize the name of Tubal-Cain."

Samuel thought for a moment. "I do recognize it. A descendant of Cain, he was a skilled worker in bronze and iron."

"And have you ever seen iron before? Ever held it?"

"No."

"You have now."

Ahitub let out a low whistle.

"These Sea People—they've rediscovered something we forgot after the Flood. Everyone I've spoken to about the Sea People have talked about this iron, and nobody seems to know how they make it. Chisda the goldsmith from the compound—he lives here as well—he doesn't know how to smelt it either.

"But people want it, boy. They've seen how tough it is. It's stronger than any other metal, certainly stronger than flint. The Sea People make their weapons from it. That's what sends some of the people here to Aphek. And they go there from Shiloh and from Lebonah and from Tappuah. They want what the Sea People have and are selling themselves to get it."

"That's not true!" Samuel protested.

"You have eyes—you can see how the bargain works. Why should the Sea People fight us when we're so willing to surrender ourselves for the sake of iron for plowshares and axheads? Why kill us when they can buy us?" he asked bitterly.

"How did you get that knife, then?"

"A tanner from here does a lot of business in Lebonah. He told me he'd gotten it in payment from someone, and he paid me with it when he took delivery on some jars. Although he told me all about it and about iron, he wasn't fool enough to tell me *where* he'd gotten it. For all I know, one of the Sea People might have been scouting up here in the hills and lost it. Or maybe he missed his footing and fell to his death and the tanner took it off the body. In any event, it's not something to brag about to just anyone."

"I understand."

"I hope you do, boy; I hope you do. The next time you hear the voice of the Lord, be sure to ask Him when we're all going to die."

If anyone else had talked that way to Samuel people might have considered it the height of blasphemy. Samuel, however, understood Issachar's ways.

Because of what they had discussed, nobody got much of a Sabbath rest that day.

It was afternoon when Samuel and Ahitub prepared to leave. "Tired of listening to an old man's words already?" Issachar asked.

"Hardly," Samuel replied. "I just want to try to make it to the home of Abinadab in Kiriath-Jearim before dark. We'll spend the night there, then head home to Ramah."

"You keep those eyes of yours open when you're that close to the foothills. It wouldn't surprise me if the Sea People aren't doing the same."

"I'll be careful, old friend," he said as he embraced Issachar farewell.

"You'll need more than that. One of these days, young seer, talk will have to give way to action. I hope neither of us live to see it."

"You just take care of yourself," the younger man replied, trying to sound braver than he felt.

"Don't worry about me—I'm used to doing that."

With that, Samuel and Ahitub turned west, heading away from the sheltered village of Shiloh. But for how long, Samuel wondered, would it remain so?

It was a long afternoon's travel, south past Bethel and Mizpah, then through Gibeon, until finally, with the ocean glinting in the distance and the sun about to set into it, they arrived at the home of Abinadab.

"You have come, seer," Abinadab said as he escorted them into the courtyard of his house. There a servant waited to wash their feet, something that had not happened to them in all of their travels, for Samuel believed that he should avoid even that rudimentary bit of hospitality in the interest of impartiality.

"Thank you, Abinadab," Samuel said; then he asked for an oil lamp. After lighting it, Samuel went around the side of Abinadab's house to an attached room with a single door. Holding the lamp near it, he inspected a spot on the door where a mud seal held in place a strip of extremely weathered cloth. Through an opening he could see an oddly shaped object beneath a covering.

Samuel sighed in relief. The ark was still safe, still locked away.

In some ways, this evening was the best one the two had spent on their journey. Abinadab invited Samuel and Ahitub into his home to share his evening meal. They slept not indoors or in their tent, but on Abinadab's roof beneath the stars, feeling the cool winds from the sea wash over them. And when they left in the morning, it was with the sense that they were almost done with their travels and would soon be home.

Samuel's thoughts, however, turned dark as he looked over his shoulder, down to the plains below. He didn't know what—and the Lord had revealed nothing to him—but something was going to happen, something serious. It might not occur the next day, or even the next year, but things could not stay as they were forever. The uneasy peace between the tribes of Israel and the Sea People was like a fragile clay jar, ready to shatter.

Part Three

"HOW I PROVIDE FOR THIS FAMILY is nobody's business, least of all *yours!*"

"How you provide for this family will end up *killing* this family!"

It was approaching midday. Samuel stood in the courtyard, undoing the ropes that held his tent and the remains of his provisions on the back of the donkey. He could hear every word, first from Shemed and then Lebiya. Sighing, he shook his head.

He had just finished another summer tour of the tribal land, making the long circuit of Bethel, Gilgal, and Mizpah where he adjudicated, taught, and preached to the people of the three towns. He had then made side trips to Shiloh to visit Issachar and then to Kiriath-Jearim to check on the ark of the covenant. It was still locked away in the house of Abinadab, still undisturbed after 20 years.

At first Samuel had been glad to catch sight of the family farmstead outside Ramah. He had traveled alone this year, as he had done most years. Ten years ago he had taken Ahitub along for company, but the next year Elkanah, under pressure from his sons by Peninah, had kept the younger brother home so that he could be of more use around the farmstead. "Better than wasting his time wandering the land with you," Shemed had sneered when Elkanah had given in and forbidden the young boy from making the rounds with Samuel a second year. Samuel had promised Ahitub that he could accompany him again the following year, but one year became two and then three, and soon it seemed as if Ahitub had forgotten all about it.

Not that he had an easier life on the farm—it seemed as if nobody did. No matter how old the children had gotten, it was an annual struggle to till and plow and plant and harvest. Elkanah did what he could, but his age was beginning to catch up to him, and he couldn't work as long and hard as before.

"He still does a better job than Samuel, though," was the inevitable taunt.

Samuel knew he couldn't avoid the confrontation much longer. Taking a deep breath, he stepped through the door.

It seemed as if everybody had gathered in the main room of the house. Shemed, Lebiya, Elkanah, and Ahitub stood facing each other, and everyone else was seated on the floor. His mother, Hannah, Samuel noted, sat with her head bowed down and her back against the wall. She was one of the few who glanced up when Samuel entered. Shemed glared at Lebiya and Ahitub, both of whom glowered back, while Elkanah seemed to wait for a break in the storm, something that he knew in his heart would never come.

"Look who's returned," Izhar loudly announced. "Our illustrious judge, finished meddling in everybody else's affairs and ready now to tell us what to do!"

Not now! Samuel thought to himself.

"Don't say one word!" Shemed threatened Samuel.

"That's right!" Lebiya shouted. "Don't say a word. But if you do, make sure the word is 'traitor'!"

That earned Lebiya a blow to the face from Shemed. She fell to the floor as if dead. Elkanah and Ahitub instantly grabbed Shemed and held him for a few seconds, until he shook them both off, roared "Leave me alone!" and stormed out of the house. Samuel helped Lebiya to her feet.

"Are you all right?" he asked.

"Why does the seer even need to ask?"

"That's enough out of you, Izhar!" Elkanah exploded.

"You're right," Izhar said as he struggled drunkenly to his feet. "That's enough out of me. That's enough out of all of us! So let's all go quietly to the slaughter like good little lambs." Before anyone could say anything else, he staggered out the door.

"Gershom," Hannah said, "make sure he gets up to the roof without breaking his neck." With that, Gershom left the room and with Izhar's arm draped across his shoulder led him up the steps to the roof of the house, where he'd gotten into the habit of sleeping.

"What happened?" Samuel finally asked.

"What we knew would happen sooner or later," Lebiya said bitterly. "Shemed's turned traitor."

"It's not treason if he only wants to—" Elkanah began.

"Wants to what—let them do whatever they want to the farm?"

"Stop it!" Samuel shouted. "Now, please, what happened?"

"I was drawing water at the well in town," Lebiya began, "and one of Nehum's servants told me that Nehum was wondering whether Shemed was going to accept Nehum's offer to borrow his plowshare after the early rains were done. I told her I didn't know anything about it; then she told me she'd heard that Shemed had his own plans and that he'd been bragging all about it two days ago, talking about how he'd had to go to Ekron for it."

"Ekron!" Samuel's eyes widened. "But that's—"

"That's right, it's one of the cities of the Sea People. He just admitted it before you came in. Shemed had taken my dowry—*my dowry*—and bought an iron plowshare!" Lebiya then ran from the room in tears.

The news stunned Samuel. He had spend the past several days in the Benjaminite cities answering questions about dealing with the Sea People. Many had a consuming desire for virtually anything made of iron, and the Sea People hadn't relaxed their monopoly on its manufacture or the sharpening of iron implements. The people of Israel were strongly divided on the subject. Some said that encouraging trade would pacify the Sea People so that they wouldn't want to conquer neighboring territories; others said that the invaders had earned their prosperity at the expense of Israel. Did Samuel have a word from the Lord on the matter?

Unfortunately, the Lord had said nothing to Samuel about it, and he had to admit as much. Although he had spent much time alone, in prayer, waiting for some sign that the Lord would give him one way or the other, nothing had happened. And now the question that was dividing the confederacy of tribes was splitting his own household. He could feel Hannah, Elkanah, and Ahitub looking at him, wondering if and how he would answer.

"Did Shemed really steal Lebiya's dowry?" he finally asked.

"All of it," Elkanah said weakly, "the entire inheritance that Peninah had promised to her before she died."

Samuel wanted to ask "How could he?" when he realized he already knew the answer to that question. Shemed did whatever he thought was right simply because he was the firstborn and because he had the strength to back up his word.

And it wasn't just Shemed. During his travels during the past few days he could feel the nation coming apart like a garment starting to rip at the seams. It made him sick at heart.

Nobody said anything—nobody knew what to say. Samuel seated himself heavily on the floor, as Hannah instructed Elisheba to bring him some food and something to drink.

"I'm not hungry," he said softly. "I just want to . . ."

Leaving the sentence unfinished, he walked out of the house. He trudged up the outside stairs to the roof of the house. Two bowers, each one a simple arrangement of four poles and branches lashed between them to fashion a rudimentary roof, had been set up there to provide shade. Izhar was lying beneath one of them with his arms outstretched, snoring loudly, sleeping off the wine. Samuel seated himself under the other bower. Drawing his knees to his chest, he bowed his head and prayed, and as he did he remembered.

"It's as bad as I've ever seen it," Issachar had said during their last visit, "and coming from me, that's saying something! What is it like at Ramah?"

"Just as bad. Everybody's worried, and nobody knows what to do. It's as if . . . as if everybody is wandering around lost, like sheep in a field when the shepherd is gone."

"Oh, but they're smart enough sheep to want one!"

"One what?"

"A shepherd. Listen to me, Samuel. Eli's been dead 20 years now, right? He may not have been much of a shepherd in Israel, but he was still there. But why am I telling you this? You know what happens when people get tired of waiting."

At first Samuel wasn't sure what Issachar meant, but then something crossed his mind (the Lord must have awakened it), for he said, "When people get tired of waiting, they make a golden calf!"

"Exactly! And Moses was gone, what, only 40 days? I'm telling you, these people have gotten tired of waiting all these years. And with no shepherd, no high priest, they'll follow anything. Even if it's only their own noses!"

"What are you saying?"

"I'm saying that maybe it's time for the Lord to put an end to the exile of the ark."

"No! That's not going to happen!"

"What's the matter with you? Haven't you given a thought to—"

"I have thought about it, Issachar!" Samuel shouted. "I wish I could forget about it, but I can't! The sanctuary was like home to me. Eli was like my own father. But the ritual service . . . even before the ark was gone I couldn't see the glory of the Lord any longer—only human corruption."

"And is that what you've heard from the Lord, a command to keep the ark locked away forever?"

"And who could be entrusted with it? The 70 men of Beth-Shemesh struck dead when the Sea People returned the ark to us? There's nobody fit to deal with the ark!"

"Except you?"

Samuel didn't have an answer to that. It hadn't occurred to him, as indignant as he was about how the Levites were no longer fit to deal with the ark, that he himself might be falling under the temptation of spiritual pride. Ashamed of himself, he bowed his head; then Issachar reached out, grazed Samuel's sleeve, finally grabbed on to it tight, as if the younger man had fallen into a well and Issachar meant to pull him out.

"Listen to me, boy. These people—these confused sheep you talk about—are going to follow a shepherd, no matter what. My ears are still good, and I've listened to what people are saying. A few want the Levitical priesthood back, a few even dare to speak of having a king over us. But most people don't know what they long for. This is a big problem, too big to keep within the lands of Benjamin."

"I don't understand."

"Don't be surprised if the Lord speaks to you once again. And you'd better be as ready to listen to Him as you were 20 years ago."

Samuel looked startled for a moment, then said, "Thank you,

Issachar. I forgot that for a moment, but you helped me remember. Thank you."

"Save your thanks. Whatever God asks of you may be the hardest thing you'll ever have to do, harder even than working that farm of yours. And one more thing: you'd better make sure that when you're ready to listen to the Lord, everyone else is ready to listen to you."

"What do you mean?"

"Do you expect me to tell you *everything?* You'll have to learn that for yourself."

It was on that note that Samuel and Issachar had parted. From there Samuel headed west to the house of Abinadab, to check on the ark.

As usual, all was secure. He found that the impromptu seal he had fixed to the door had remained undisturbed, and he could see through a crack in the door that the ark was still there.

"Excuse me?"

Samuel turned around. Eleazar, son of Abinadab, anointed by Samuel to safeguard the ark, stood behind him.

"Yes, what is it?"

"Well, I was just wondering, if it's not too much trouble . . ."

"You're wondering what's going to happen to the ark?"

Eleazar nodded.

"I wish I could tell you, but I don't know yet. But when God does *tell* me, you'll be the first to hear."

"Thank you. It's just that my brother came to help with the grain harvest and his son was asking about the ark: what it looks like, does it do anything—you know, the questions children raise. I must've looked pretty foolish when I told him I didn't know anything about it."

"How old is the boy?"

"Three years. You know how they are at that age. A cousin of mine tried to answer the boy's questions, but he wasn't much help. He was only just born when you had the ark placed here. He's gone his whole life with the ark of the covenant shut up in one room of our house—can you imagine?"

"Yes," Samuel replied, his face reddening. "I have . . . a brother who's your cousin's age."

Abinadab's hospitality was as good as it always was, and Samuel should have been grateful for it. But something about Eleazar's words stuck with him. They'd weighed on him all through the journey from Beth-Shemesh back home to Ramah. And now, up on the roof of his own house, they pressed down on him like millstones.

It wasn't just a matter of Ahitub and others his age having grown up without seeing the ark. Samuel had lived next to it in the tabernacle for eight years and had never seen it himself. The only person who had seen it was Eli, and then only once a year. But then Hophni and Phinehas had taken it away . . .

It always came back to that for Samuel: Hophni and Phinehas. Eli may have enfeebled the Levitical priesthood, but his two sons had thoroughly corrupted it. That was why Samuel's anger had flared when he was talking with Issachar. He couldn't bear the thought of calling for the resurrection of the priesthood, even if enough Levites still lived to resume the ancient rites. He didn't want to see the old evil reborn.

He sat up, then stood. From the roof of the house he could look out over the fields—fields that would be tilled with the iron plowshare of the Sea People. And there was no use trying to talk Shemed into changing his mind. Samuel had recognized from the tone in his brother's voice that he wasn't about to return the plowshare. It was too important to him and his idea of how the farm should be run. It was like . . .

. . . an idol. An idol made of iron!

Samuel walked down the stairs to the ground and headed toward the vines the family kept, because it was still the time of the tending of summer fruits. He caught up with Shemed as he was preparing to trim some vines trailing on the ground.

"Shemed!" he called out. Slowly the half brother straightened up.

"What?" he growled.

"Where's the plowshare?"

"What's it to you?"

"It's going back."

"You're dreaming," he said, and turned back to his work. Whether possessed by God or by some other spirit, Samuel caught him by the upper arm and forced him to turn and face him.

"It's going back. You stole from your own sister to get it, and you have to make restitution."

"I don't have to make anything," Shemed hissed as he brandished a flint pruning knife close to Samuel's face. "And you can't make me return it, either."

"Then I'll return it myself."

"You? Go to the Sea People? You are crazy!"

"It's going back," Samuel replied in a steady voice.

"For what?" Shemed exploded. "To get back a dowry for a sister who isn't even betrothed yet and probably never will be? It was going to waste anyway! At least the plowshare will be of some use around here, which is more than I can say for her. Or for you!"

"It's going back."

Shemed gripped the pruning knife so hard his knuckles whitened. Had Samuel noticed it he might have been frightened, but he held his ground. It may have been Samuel's resolve, or it may have been the last burning ember of guilt in Shemed at having stolen his own sister's dowry, but Shemed's hand began to tremble. It was barely noticeable at first, but soon it became more violent, until simply to stop it from shaking he jammed the knife into the thick vine.

"Fine! Go on!" he screamed. "Return it if that'll shut you up!" Then, his back to Samuel, he began to vent his anger on the vine.

★   ★   ★

It did not take Samuel long to find the plowshare in the outbuilding where they kept the other farm implements. Shemed had wrapped it in a goatskin and placed it in the bottom half of a broken storage jar. Removing it, Samuel unwound the skin and examined the metal object in the light filtering through the open doorway.

Samuel was the last person in the world to be impressed by any farm implement. It simply reminded him of all the hard work that went into running the place. Yet even he couldn't fail to appreciate the new plowshare. Designed to fit onto the plow shaft, it was large and heavy, heavier than if it had been made of bronze, and there was something almost hypnotic about its dull gleaming surface.

Samuel shook his head to refocus his thoughts. The plowshare also represented Lebiya's dowry. That made it far more important than any value it had as a farm tool. Shemed could find some other way to get a new plowshare if he wanted it badly enough.

It was a good distance to Ekron, Samuel knew as he set out, the skin-wrapped plowshare tied to his donkey. He might possibly get as far as Beth-Shemesh by dark if he made good time. If not, he would have to spend the night in Kiriath-Jearim. It wasn't until later that afternoon, when he was halfway between Gibeon and Kiriath-Jearim, that he realized that he hadn't brought any food with him. He'd been that upset with Shemed's bartering away Lebiya's dowry. But it was too late to turn back. Although he wasn't sure what he'd do about feeding himself, he kept on.

Near Kiriath-Jearim he stopped. He was close to the edge of the highlands now. To have continued on would have meant descending the foothills. Feeling fatigued, he bowed to the inevitable and went to the home of Abinadab. Although he hated to presume upon the man's hospitality so soon since his last visit, he had little choice.

As it turned out, he needn't have worried. Abinadab graciously received him and showed him the same courtesy he always had. Relaxed and well fed, Samuel then followed him to the guest chamber on the roof of the house where he would spend the night.

But Samuel couldn't sleep. No matter how he tried, it wouldn't come. Finally, after tossing on his blanket, he felt his way down the stairs and stopped before the door that led into the room housing the ark. There he rested his forehead against the wood.

"Lord," he whispered, "I don't know what to do. I'm doing this because I want to do what's right in Your sight and not my own. But how can I start to do that when I can't know what . . .

"No, I *do* know what's wrong. Your people have forgotten You. And it shows in more ways than just trading with the Sea People. But I can't see clearly what needs to be done or what it would take to accomplish it. I need help to see it, please!"

His eyes still closed, he raised his head. A cool breeze from the sea swept his hair back. There was something assuring about it, even if he still didn't know what the Lord meant him to do for His people.

One thing at a time, Samuel thought. *First the plowshare.*

★   ★   ★

The journey down from Kiriath-Jearim to Beth-Shemesh and from there to the foothill city of Timnah was far more agreeable than that from Jerusalem to Jericho. Although still a considerable descent, it had none of the oppressive mugginess of the Jordan Valley. This air was bracing and pleasant—almost uncomfortably pleasant.

Abinadab had told him that he would need to inquire at Timnah the way to Ekron, for the man never went below Beth-Shemesh. He also advised Samuel that he was wasting his time and would be better off going back to Ramah. But Samuel had made up his mind. As he neared Timnah, he looked up and down the verdant coastal plain and out toward the sea. It all seemed so peaceful. His mind told him to ignore that impression, to remember that the Sea People ruled the area now.

Suddenly someone looming up in front of him interrupted his thoughts. The man was such a frightening figure that Samuel was speechless. Tall, bare-chested, and built like a stone pillar, the individual wore a simple skirt that went from his waist to his knees. He also wore a bronze circlet on his head, from which horsehairs stood up straight like wheat in a field. A long spear was strapped to his back, and bronze plating of some kind covered his shins. Now he drew his sword from its sheath. "State your business!" he ordered in an accented voice.

"I'm . . . going to Ekron."

"What for?"

"I need to return something."

"What?"

Reluctantly Samuel unwrapped the skin and showed the plowshare to the man, who was apparently one of the Sea People. After glancing at it, the warrior then waved a similarly dressed companion of his over to look at it as well. They took it off the donkey, hefted it in their hands, and looked admiringly at it from every angle. After conferring with each other in low voices, they returned the plowshare to him.

"Why do you want to return it? What's wrong with it?"

"Nothing's . . . wrong with it. I need to get back the payment given for it, that's all."

The two Sea People muttered together some more before breaking out into raucous laughter. Samuel didn't know which was worse: that he was somehow the butt of some joke, or that he was unable to understand the humor.

"Follow us," the first man said, and after replacing the plowshare, Samuel began to accompany the men on the road to Ekron.

"Where did you get that?"

"I didn't," Samuel replied. "My brother did."

"Brothers!" he laughed derisively, then turned and spoke to his companion. Once more they enjoyed a good laugh for reasons that Samuel couldn't understand.

It wasn't long before they approached the city of Ekron. By now the guards almost completely ignored Samuel, but as they neared the city, they glanced back at him and stopped. Samuel stood staring at the city, transfixed.

"What do you see?" the guard asked.

Samuel said nothing.

"You've never seen it before?"

"I . . . I have seen it before," he answered, his voice subdued.

"Does it make you afraid?" the guard asked. His companion's brow was furrowed.

"Not the city, no, but I . . . I've seen it before, but I can't remember . . ."

"How can you not remember? You saw it or you—"

"Mice!"

"What mice? Where?" Both guards looked around their feet, as if expecting to see rodents scampering over them.

"Twenty years ago. I saw the fields outside this city overrun by mice."

"You saw them? You were here?"

"No. I've never been here. I just . . . *saw* them."

The two guards huddled once more. This time they discussed something with each other for quite a while, gesturing animatedly. Finally the first guard turned to Samuel. "He'll take you where you're going. We know who made that." Then, without another word, he walked away. The other guard silently motioned for Samuel to keep moving.

It was only as Samuel entered the city in the company of the second guard that he realized that he might have placed himself in jeopardy. He had admitted to having viewed Ekron in vision, one of the five cities where the Sea People had held the ark of the covenant before returning it. Now he dared say nothing more, especially about seeing the tumors in vision as well. Quickly he sent up a prayer to God, not knowing into what danger he had chosen to walk.

Just then the Sea People warrior gestured for him to go to the right, toward a small cluster of buildings attached to the city wall. Samuel nodded in response and guided the donkey toward them.

As he approached, the most unusual smell hit him. It was something he'd never fully encountered before. He knew the scent of molten metal, for back at the sanctuary compound he had passed the tent of Chisda the goldsmith more than once. And he was also only too familiar with the odor of fire from working near the altar of sacrifice.

But this was different. It was partly the smell of fire, but definitely not as clean. Nor was it the aroma of cooking. It was heavy, faintly reminding him of the clouds that brought the early rains, and it also had a tinge of earth, but not of soil freshly turned by a plow. It was a stench that seemed to grab Samuel by the throat and threatened to choke the life from him.

The guard then pointed Samuel toward a small knot of men outside the buildings. Taking the plowshare, he approached them. They all looked like farmers to Samuel.

"Back to the end!" one of the men shouted. "Wait your turn like everyone else."

When Samuel started to apologize, another man interrupted: "Wait! Come here." Samuel walked up to him.

"Are you the seer?" he asked in a low voice, glancing about as he spoke.

"I am Samuel, son of Elkanah."

"I thought so. Abinadab of Beth-Shemesh is my father. I saw you the last time you were at his house. What are you doing here?"

"I'm returning something. Why are you here?"

In answer, the man undid a small bundle of cloth that held a small axhead made of iron.

"It's gotten dull. I have to come here to have them sharpen it. I wish I knew how so I could do it myself."

"Greedy, every one of them," another farmer muttered. "They know they've got hold of us by the neck."

"How many of you come to Ekron?"

"It's easier to say how many don't. Somehow or other we all rely on what they have, even if we're paying through the nose for it now."

Samuel started to say something, but a gesture from the farmer silenced him. The other guard approached in the company of an older man. Samuel guessed that he was close to Elkanah's age. The individual's fine clothes reminded Samuel for a moment of the garments of the high priest Eli. The Sea People official walked up to Samuel.

"Why are you here?" he asked, his accent barely detectable.

"I want to return something. A plowshare. My brother bought it with his sister's dowry."

"That is a problem, isn't it?" the man said, though the tone of his voice made him sound as if he were complaining about a dab of mud on his fine cloak. "Come along." The official headed toward the front of the line.

The guard nudged Samuel. "Follow."

Samuel took the plowshare, looking apologetically at the men standing outside.

Inside the first building it was like an oven. A piece of fabric separated the chamber from a second one in back. Two other guards stood by the door. One was drinking water from a skin. He passed it to his fellow, who poured some over his head instead of drinking it. It mingled with the sweat rolling down his bare chest.

A second later the curtain swung aside and a man appeared. He too was stripped to the waist and sweating. Seeing the finely dressed official, he bowed.

"What do you wish of me, *seren* [warlord]?" he asked. His voice was deep and husky, and the smell of smoke clung to him.

"You sold a plowshare to this man," he began.

"To my brother, actually," Samuel interrupted. "Taller than I am, a bit older. Name's Shemed."

"What about it?"

"He wants to return it," the official explained, "and he wants you to give back what you took for it."

"Is there a problem with my work?"

"No, no," Samuel hastened to say. The heat in the small room was the worst he'd ever experienced. He wanted this to be over as soon as possible so he could go outside and breathe again. "But I need to get back what he gave you for it—it was my sister's dowry."

The blacksmith frowned. "Well, that's different. Let me see."

Samuel handed over the skin, and the man unwrapped it.

"Oh, yes, I remember this one," he said. He hefted the plowshare with his muscular arms as if it weighed no more than a loaf of bread. "Good piece of work went into that, too. And I remember whom I sold it to. Wasn't in a mood to haggle, as I recall. Everything should still be at my home, if my wife hasn't bartered it away by now," he added with a laugh.

"Yes," the warlord said dryly. "Bring them around to the palace as soon as you can."

"Yes, *seren*."

"And as for you," he said as he turned to Samuel, "we need to talk."

★   ★   ★

The "palace" of the *seren* wasn't the tallest building in Ekron, but it was certainly the most spacious. Samuel realized that his own house could have fit inside it with ease. Here the warlord showed Samuel hospitality by having his feet washed and giving him food and a place to rest until the blacksmith arrived with the dowry.

Samuel wanted to be gracious in accepting what the *seren* offered, but he was also wary. He was in the hands of the Sea People, after all, and must have passed a dozen armed guards before he had arrived at the room they were in. They could very well take him captive at any moment. That they hadn't already done so he attributed to the Lord's providence.

"Are you sure you won't have some?" the *seren* asked after Samuel had refused, for the third time, to accept any wine. "It's quite good, you know."

"Thank you again, but I cannot."

"Then may I ask why? I get the feeling that you mistrust either my wine or myself. Which is it?"

"Neither. I refrain because of a vow made to my God."

"Ah," the *seren* replied, drawing out the word as he spoke it. "I have heard that the hills are a hard and rough country. Is your God the same?"

"No, it's not like that. It was a vow of dedication to the Lord. As long as I was to be in His service I was not to cut my hair, and I was not to partake of grapes or of anything made from grapes."

"Yes, yes, the business about the hair. I remember hearing about one of your kinsmen who was like that. Supposed to have been incredibly strong."

"That would be Samson, son of Manoah."

"From what I hear, he wasn't as particular about wine as you are."

Suddenly Samuel felt uneasy, like a sheep that had just realized that it was being watched by a wolf. "He served the Lord as well as he could, and I serve Him as well as I can."

"And that includes your going around to various cities as a seer."

"Yes."

"And what is it that you proclaim?"

"Obedience to the Lord and to His law."

"Anything else?"

"I don't understand." He thought he did, however.

"One of the guards who brought you to the city was under the impression that you foresaw the devastation of our city 20 years ago."

"He thought that because I told him that I had seen it."

"And you didn't think to tell us?"

"I was only 12 years old at the time. Besides, I'd never even seen Ekron until today!"

"Except in your vision, of course. Tell me," he said as he took up an elegant bronze knife and began toying with it idly, "do you think we deserved what happened to us? Or any of the other four cities?"

"It's not for me to say one way or the other. What happened came to pass because the ark of the covenant had been brought to the cities. It was the Lord who acted, and it is not my place to question His deeds."

The *seren* seemed to ponder Samuel's answer for a few seconds, still twisting the dagger as he did so. Finally he placed it back on the table before him. "Fair enough. Well, I think it's time we took our rest. Let me show you to your quarters."

The room where he took Samuel was the opposite of his home in Ramah. Where that house was dark and cramped even in the large front room, this chamber was airy and open and comfortable. "When the dowry arrives, I'll have it sent to you."

"Thank you," Samuel replied.

The *seren* then left him and returned to the main room. A soldier waited for him, a grizzled veteran of high rank and as old as the *seren* himself.

"Well?" the warrior asked.

"He claims that he didn't know anything about the plagues, that he was only a boy when they struck."

"And you believe him?"

"He's certainly young enough—of course I believe him. That does not mean, however, that I trust him. Please, let's be seated.

"I have no idea what he does. His hands tell me he's just another farmer from the hill country. His words, however, suggest something else."

"I've questioned some of the Hill People, as you asked," the soldier said. "Some of them have heard of him; others haven't."

"And those who have heard of him, what do they have to say?"

"You know how it is with these Hill People—can't get a straight answer out of any of them. But I get the feeling that they respect him."

"Then I think it may be time that they learned to respect us as well. Someone like this seer could rouse the Hill People against us. Such things have happened before. Besides, my elder brother died here during the plague, so I have a score to settle with their God.

"Select the best men of your garrison, train them hard, then choose one of their cities in the hills and raze it to the ground. It doesn't have to be a large city, just big enough that its fall will send a message to the Hill People that their God isn't as powerful as they think."

"Yes, *seren.*"

"One more thing: don't tell me where or when you plan to attack."

"I understand, *seren.* I already have a city in mind."

★　★　★

"You're leaving *again?*"

"Yes, Ahitub." Samuel checked the meager provisions one more time before lashing them to the donkey's back.

"But you only just got back with Lebiya's dowry."

"That was two months ago."

"And it's almost time for the olive harvest. I know you don't like the work, but . . ."

"It's not about the work, it's . . . I just feel I have to go back to the cities and give them a message."

"What message?"

"That the only way we're going to be delivered from the hand of the Sea People is if we return to the Lord and put away all other gods."

"Who said anything about even wanting to be delivered?" Shemed interrupted. He had barely spoken two words to Samuel since he had returned with Lebiya's dowry. "We're safe enough up here in the hills."

"But for how long?" Ahitub asked. "People say that the Sea People are getting stronger."

"Getting fatter is more like it."

"Yes, by eating the food grown on land taken from us!"

"All right," Elkanah said as he walked out, "we're not going to start that argument again. Samuel, your mother wants to see you before you leave."

Samuel found Hannah inside, lying down where she usually slept. She had taken ill two days before, and Jedidah, her youngest daughter, now attended her.

"Leave us, please," she asked Jedidah.

"Yes, Mother."

"Samuel," Hannah asked when they were alone, "do you still plan to go to the cities with this message?"

"Yes, I do."

"Then I must ask you a question. Don't answer it; just let me ask it: Is this message from the Lord, and are you prepared to listen to it yourself?"

It so reminded him of the question that Issachar had put to him that there was no way he could regard it as anything but God's providence. Samuel wanted to blurt out "Of course!" but something about the look in her eyes prevented him from saying a word. Even if she hadn't told him not to answer, something about the question cut through him the way an ax does through a tree. He was barely able to tell her "I'll be back as soon as I can" before kissing her, rising to his feet, then calling Jedidah back into the room. He didn't say anything to Elkanah, Shemed, or Ahitub as he left a few moments later.

★ ★ ★

Two days later, at the gate of Gilgal, Samuel had delivered the same message he had given at Bethel the day before.

"There are those who will tell you that the glory of Israel has departed because of the presence of the Sea People. That's not true. For I saw the glory of Israel depart myself.

"It was many years ago. The sons of the high priest Eli had convinced the people that if they brought the ark of the covenant into battle against the Sea People, then Israel would surely be victorious. And the people believed them.

"So they did just that. They entered the Most Holy Place, forbidden to all except the high priest, and removed the ark. Then they carried it to Aphek, the site of a great skirmish they were fighting against the Sea People. Yet despite their plans the sons of Eli perished on the field of battle that day, and the Sea People captured the ark.

"You have been told what happened next, and I have seen it in vision: how plagues like those that fell on Egypt also struck the cities of the Sea People. So devastating were they that the Sea People sent the ark back to us and it remains safe to this day.

"But when it arrived back, it was as if someone had returned a lamp that could no longer give light. For though they returned the ark, the glory of the Lord did not return with it.

"The ark was where the shekinah, the glory of the Lord, dwelt. But when the ark came back to us, there was as much death and misery among us as there was among the Sea People.

"Why? Because for too long we have forsaken the God who

brought us out of Egypt, and followed other gods. For too long we have exchanged the slavery of Egypt for the slavery of these other gods.

"And now we are making ourselves slaves all over again. We do it by forsaking the way of the Lord our God and following after the Baals and Ashtoreths and their perverse rites." Samuel didn't want to say any more about such ceremonies, and he didn't need to. They knew if only by hearsay about the belief that ritualistic copulation would bring about an abundant harvest.

"We do it by conceding to the Sea People the land that was promised to the tribe of Judah. We do it by our own day-to-day forsaking of the Lord and of His law.

"And what is to be done? The answer doesn't lie in rebuilding the tabernacle, for it never stopped anyone from sinning. It doesn't lie with the Levites at all—it lies with you. Return to the Lord with all your hearts. Put away the foreign gods from among you, and prepare your heart for the Lord, the one true God, and serve Him only. Then He will deliver you from the hands of the Sea People!"

Many in the crowd were visibly moved. So why did it feel as if something was wrong? Samuel wondered that evening as he sat before his tent, eating the meager ration he had set for himself.

Try as he might, he could not lose the sound of his mother's words: that he should be prepared to listen to his own message. Yet he wasn't sure exactly what she meant. Perhaps there was something wrong in his own life, something that could not respond to what he had been saying. But what? If anything, he was as overobservant of the law as the sons of Peninah alleged. Despite the death of Eli, he had not believed himself to be released from the particulars of the vow of a Nazirite to which his mother had bound him before his birth. To abandon it now, for whatever reason, seemed to him to be the height of apostasy, as wrong as the abduction of the ark by Hophni and Phinehas.

No! he told himself. It wasn't the same thing at all. He followed the life of a Nazirite in all its austerity in service to the Lord, not to curry anybody's favor. Hophni and Phinehas had lived for themselves. There was no similarity, he told himself—it was the difference between east and west!

Whether it was the oppressive heat and humidity of the Jordan

Valley even in late summer, or whether the past two days of hard travel and exhortation had finally caught up with him, Samuel found his eyes growing heavy. Deciding not to fight it, he went into his tent and slept.

It seemed to be only a short time later that Samuel sensed light streaming into his tent from outside. But there was something strange, lurid about it, as if it were the wrong color. Curious, he looked outside.

What he saw made him gasp. Fire seemed to surround him. It was not a solid wall of flame, though. Here and there spots burned as if from pitch oozing up from the ground. Gilgal was ablaze, smoke rolling above the city and into the sky, hiding the sun. There was nothing clean about this smoke, as with the incense clouds at the sanctuary or even the smoke that rose from the altar of sacrifice. He glanced toward Jerusalem and saw the same sickly smoke ascending from it. Occasional cries and screams only served to underscore the deathly silence behind everything.

Just then Samuel felt a hand grasping his shoulder. He froze, knowing, without looking or being told, that it was a dead man's hand that had seized him. His insides curdled and churned. Despite being surrounded by flames, he suddenly felt colder than he ever had in his life. Yet he also felt that he had to find out who was touching him. He turned his head and confronted a figure with a hooded head. Then a burst of flame nearby illuminated the being's face, and Samuel realized that it was Issachar, his mouth open in a silent scream. He raised an iron dagger as if to strike Samuel.

Bolting upright, Samuel was breathing hard, and sweat poured from him. Burying his face in his hands, he simply begged God to be near him. He didn't know why he prayed that prayer—it was the only thing that he could think to ask of the Lord at that moment. He waited until his heart beat more normally. It had been a long time since he had had dreams like this one. It reminded him of those that he realized much later had foretold the fall of . . .

That's when Samuel realized that he heard voices. They had an urgency about them that was unlike the casual conversation he heard at the city gates. Bracing himself for the worst, he looked outside his tent.

Outside there was no conflagration, no flame-blasted landscape.

But a crowd with lamps and torches had assembled at the gate of Gilgal. Yet it was long past the time that the gates would have been closed for the evening. Something was wrong.

"Seer!" someone called from nearby, and a young man ran up to the tent.

"What's wrong?" Samuel asked.

The youth took a minute to catch his breath. "I've been sent to get you. Come at once! Please!"

The man didn't explain why, and Samuel was afraid to ask. He nodded and headed for the city gate. There he found that a shepherd was the center of everyone's attention. He seemed unnaturally pale, even in the torchlight that bathed him.

"Make way! The seer is here!" the young person that had fetched Samuel called out, leading him to the shepherd.

"What happened?" Samuel asked.

"Yes, tell him what you told us!" someone shouted from the crowd.

"I . . . I don't know where to . . ."

"Don't be afraid," Samuel said, as much to himself as to the shepherd. "Tell me what you saw."

"My father and I were moving our flock south to Arumah last night. We'd come to some grazing land just north of Shiloh. There we had settled the flock for the evening when they became alert and worried. At first we thought there might be an animal nearby. My father told me to scout around and make sure while he stayed with the flock.

"I was looking below, into the valley where Shiloh was located. I didn't see any animals, but I did see torches, many torches, moving up the valley. I didn't dare call out—I was afraid I'd give away my hiding place if I did!

"As I watched, they . . . they fell upon the village. They burned what they could. The cries that rose up, they were . . ."

"I know what they were like," Samuel said quietly.

"Too soon everything fell silent. Then the torches headed back south down the valley, then turned to the west. I went back and told my father. He told me to go down into the village and see if anyone was left and find out what had happened.

"I went. It . . . nobody was left alive, nobody! I looked all around. I couldn't tell who had done this or why."

"Did they leave any weapons behind?"

"I did find one. An old blind man had a knife thrust into him. Whoever stabbed him just left it there."

"Where is it?"

"I brought it with me," he said as he reached into his shoulder bag and, trembling, held the knife toward Samuel. He really didn't need to say anything more to Samuel, who recognized the glare of firelight against iron.

★   ★   ★

"Are they still there?" Lebiya asked.

"They're still out there," Elisheba answered. "Looks like more today than yesterday."

Samuel had returned to Ramah after hearing what the shepherd had to say. When he arrived he didn't say a word to anyone. Instead he lay down on his bed and almost never left it for the next seven days and nights. During that time he didn't eat, drink, or speak to anyone. By now Elkanah and everyone at Ramah had heard of the raid on Shiloh, an attack that could have been carried out only by the Sea People.

Shemed and the other sons of Peninah claimed that it didn't matter to them what Samuel did, Izhar adding that Samuel could die for all he cared, just so long as he wasn't in anybody's way while he did it. But almost nobody took note of his remark. For the thing people had been dreading, the private fear of so many of the Israelites for so long, had finally come to pass: the Sea People had left the coastal plains and struck into the heart of the highlands.

A day after Samuel's return and two days after the attack, Lebiya had noticed early in the morning that someone had pitched a tent a distance from the house. It was unusual, but she didn't think much of it. Shemed guessed that it was refugees who had lived near Shiloh and were now traveling south—that they'd pull up stakes and move on later in the day. In fact, the opposite happened. Two dozen other tents joined it during the day, and another five dozen the day after

that. For the week that Samuel lay in bed without speaking to anyone, a virtual city of tents had sprung up around Elkanah's home.
Or, to be more specific, the home of the seer in Ramah.

Shemed and his brothers berated Samuel for taking to bed instead of dealing with the people congregated outside the house,
which to them meant sending the strangers away. Hannah could do
little herself other than having her children do what they could to
help and to explain that yes, Samuel was home, but no, they didn't
know whether he would see or speak to anyone today.

Then, after a week's seclusion, a gaunt and bleary-eyed Samuel,
his clothes torn as a sign of mourning, emerged from the house. His
family had told him that people had gathered to ask him what should
be done. They had come from all over Israel, from north of Shiloh
and south of Jerusalem. Now they watched and waited silently as
Samuel weakly left the courtyard of his father's house and surveyed
the field of people waiting for him. It reminded him very much of
the crowd that had assembled at the sanctuary once a year on the
Day of Atonement.

The Day of Atonement. Something about it stuck in his mind.
It was a time of repentance and humility before God, one that Israel
had not observed since the fall of the sanctuary and the capture of
the ark. Maybe now . . .

As people began crowding around him, talking at once, pouring
out streams of excited words, battling with each other to make
themselves heard, the sound interrupted his thoughts.

"Please, please!" Samuel managed to say. At once, those close to
him lapsed into silence, and it spread through the crowd like a rip-
ple in a pond.

"What do you want of me?" he asked, genuinely unsure as to
what to do, for the Lord had been silent the past seven days. In answer, an old woman stepped forward and took one of Samuel's
hands in her own. She started to say something, then stopped, apparently collecting her thoughts. He and the people around her
waited patiently. Finally, her eyes moist with tears, she said, "Please,
pray for us!"

Those few words seemed to reflect the feeling of the heart of
Israel. They had forgotten the Lord so thoroughly and for so long

that they didn't even know how to approach God, much less to ask anything of Him. But they believed Samuel did know and saw in him their only hope. Samuel, understanding this as well, accepted the burden as being from the Lord.

As weak as he was from not eating and from mourning for the dead of Shiloh, his strength seemed to grow as he surveyed the crowd. "Have you here put away the Ashtoreths and other false gods?" Samuel called out, his voice stronger than even he had thought possible.

"Yes!" many of the people answered.

"Will you serve the Lord and Him only?"

Again the crowd shouted its affirmation.

Samuel's family watched in amazement. Ahitub, standing on the roof of the house, felt a surge of admiration for his brother and the way he conducted himself before the people, more people than he had ever seen him address at any one time in the journey he remembered. The sons of Peninah were clearly irritated not so much by what was going on but by the fact that the half brother they considered to be a nobody now commanded a degree of respect that they would never know. As for Hannah, she viewed events in a spirit of quiet gratitude.

"Then gather all Israel to Mizpah, and there I will pray for you."

"When?" someone in the crowd blurted out.

"On the tenth day of the next month." It would not only give the people time to assemble; it would also coincide with the day of Atonement.

For some of the people, just knowing that the seer had spoken and that he had a plan of some sort was enough. Others began pressing toward him, to touch or, at the very least, to see him. They sought no grand strategy and asked nothing more than simple assurance, the way that a child's fear brought on by a bad dream is dispelled when someone brings a lamp into the room. Samuel could do that at the very least.

Finally, the last person had spoken to Samuel, and the tents that people had set up began to disappear quietly. Samuel turned back toward the house. As he passed Shemed he heard him mutter, "Well, *that's* over, anyway!"

Whether out of hope or guesswork, Lebiya was standing just inside the doorway with a bowl of food and some bread for Samuel. Smiling, he accepted it, then sat down and began to eat.

"What happened out there?" she asked.

"I told them to gather at Mizpah on the tenth day of next month."

"As long as they don't gather here," Izhar added.

Lebiya ignored him. "Why Mizpah?"

"It's the city in this area with the strongest defenses. If we need to, we can go inside the city walls."

"Are you expecting the Sea People to attack again?" Elkanah asked.

"I don't know. But they'll probably notice large groups of people headed toward Mizpah, even if they don't know what for. I hope they don't use it as an opportunity to attack, but I just want to make sure that nobody . . ." Letting the thought go unfinished, he picked up a piece of bread, as if to dip it into the stew in his bowl, but then just let it fall into his food.

"Samuel," Hannah said as she sat near him and put one hand on his arm, "there was nothing you could have done to save Shiloh or the people in it. As hard as it is to hear, you must believe it."

"I know, Mother, but . . . but surely there could have been some . . ."

"No, Samuel," she continued, her voice as quiet as the grave, "there was nothing. You can't blame yourself or anyone else for what was in the Lord's hand."

"But why?" Ahitub asked. "Why did it happen if it was in the Lord's hand?" Genuine anguish echoed in his voice. Had Shemed or Izhar asked that same question the tone would have been one of contempt, but they said nothing. Instead they waited to hear an explanation.

"I cannot answer that," Hannah said at last. "I am not the Lord."

"I just can't forget the horror of what I saw," Samuel said as he set his bowl down in front of him, its contents only half eaten. "The vision that I had just before I heard the news from Shiloh was too terrible to forget. How could the Lord have something like that in His hand?"

Hannah looked into her son's eyes. "Sometimes what is in the Lord's hand and what is in the Lord's heart seem like two different things. We have to trust in the one, even if all we can see is the other."

A heavy silence filled the room, broken as Samuel sighed, then ran the back of his hand across his eyes and whispered, "Thank you, Mother." Then he resumed eating—suddenly he found that his appetite had returned.

★ ★ ★

The *seren* of Ekron entered the main room of his dwelling to greet his visitor. He was not in a friendly mood, however, for he hadn't any use for the Hill People. Still, the blacksmith had sent word to him that the peasant had something important to tell him. *It had better be worth it,* he thought, *to demand to see me during midday.*

He seated himself before his visitor, who remained standing. "I'm told you have something to tell me."

"For a price."

"If it's worth hearing, you shall have it."

"Three days ago the seer of Ramah told a crowd of people to assemble next month at Mizpah, on the tenth day."

"Do you know why?"

"He said that it was for worship, that he would be praying for them."

"And you think it might be something else?"

"That I can't say. But he hopes to have people gathered there from all over Israel."

The *seren* called for a map. He studied it as the man pointed out the Aijalon Valley. "If you come up this valley here, and march this way south of Beth-Horon, you should reach it without any difficulty."

"You're being extremely helpful," the *seren* said with an edge to his voice. "How do I know that you aren't giving us false information? that you aren't yourself in league with the seer?"

"He doesn't see the same things I do."

"And what is it that you see?"

"I see the real world. I see who has the strength and the tools to make something of this land."

"And to make something of oneself?"

"It won't happen by praying to gods or lying with women."

"Then we see the same thing," the *seren* said with a smile. "And you shall be rewarded, *after* we have further convinced the Hill People that we are their overlords."

"There's only one thing I want, and I want it now."

"You're not in much of a position to insist on anything."

"I'd just as soon have it in my hands before the early rains arrive."

"You have a very practical mind—I like that. Very well. Your information is worth at least that much."

Without another word the *seren* drafted a message that he gave to the farmer standing before him. The man took it to the blacksmith and used it to redeem an iron plowshare that had lain in the workshop, unused and unsold, for almost two months.

Whatever else was going to happen in the land, Shemed thought, he had gotten what he wanted.

★　★　★

The first of the early rains had come by the time the new month rolled around. It was only enough to begin to break up the hard summer ground. But few farmers failed to take to their fields with oxen to begin turning the earth for the first planting. Shemed was one of them, and Elkanah and the others couldn't help noticing that he was using what appeared to be the same iron plowshare that had been such a point of contention before. When asked how he had come to possess it, the most he would say was "I didn't steal anything from anybody, if that's what you mean." In the face of other questions he would become sullen, then defensive, finally angry. It didn't take long for everyone to give up and let him plow.

Samuel didn't even bother asking. Instead, he spent even more time alone than usual, either walking through bare and unplowed fields or else on the roof of the house gazing off into the distance.

Coming down from the roof one afternoon, he found Hannah standing in the doorway, watching Jedidah milking their goats.

"Are you all right, Mother?"

"Yes, dear. I just wanted to get some fresh air. I really am fine!" she said as Samuel gave her a penetrating look.

"I hope so. I hate to think that something could happen to you while I'm at Mizpah."

"I'll be fine, really. If you should worry about anyone, it should be yourself."

"Why? Have you had a dream?"

"No. But I'm worried just the same."

"About the Sea People?"

"No, about Israel. I worry that they may come to expect much from you. Our people have had many *shoftim*. Some of them . . . Gideon, Jephthah . . . fought against the Sea People. They became men of blood."

"But if that's what the Lord called them to be . . ."

"And look what it did to Jephthah! He caused his own daughter to be sacrificed as easily as if she were a lamb."

"Mother," he said as he laid his hands on her shoulders, "I promise you before God, wherever the Lord directs my path I won't become a man of blood."

Hannah looked up into his face and smiled. "Thank you," she said finally.

Samuel put his arms around her and held her. As he did so, he breathed a silent prayer to God that no matter what happened at Mizpah he would keep that promise.

★   ★   ★

It was almost dawn on the tenth day of the month. Samuel had been up for much of the night. Even if Israel did not observe the Day of Atonement anymore, he could not break the habit. He had spent much of the previous night on the roof of the house, doing what he had done for the last few years he had spent at the sanctuary: rehearsing the words of the law of Moses in order to make sure Eli knew them, and to keep himself awake. Now he surprised himself by how much of the rite he still remembered. He remembered not only the words but the actions as he paced back and forth from one end of the roof to the other, between the altar and the sanctuary. All the sights and sounds and sensations from that vanished place flooded back into him as he rehearsed the rites of forgiveness and cleansing. Once more he could feel the heat of the altar of sacrifice, again smell the unmistakable mixture of blood and incense.

It gave him a certain sense of satisfaction. The sanctuary itself might be gone, Eli and his sons might be dead 20 years, but if only in his own heart it all continued, it still lived on. Perhaps it was what the Lord had meant all along, he thought. Perhaps all those who had participated in the service of the sanctuary were to make it a part of themselves and communicate it to others . . .

No. That's not how it worked, he realized. That was certainly not what had happened with the Levites of Beth-Shemesh. Their own deaths from their disrespect of the ark was proof enough of that.

Such unresolved thoughts were still whirling in his mind as he quietly prepared to leave for Mizpah. He tied his provisions onto the donkey, getting ready to leave as soon as it was light. As he did so, he was aware of a stirring inside the house. The next thing he knew, Lebiya and Ahitub were coming out of the house, each carrying a small bag.

"What are you doing?"

"Going with you, of course," Ahitub replied.

"You weren't thinking of traveling alone, were you?" Lebiya asked.

"I was, but . . . you never said anything until now."

"You never asked us, either," Ahitub said. "We know you've had a lot on your mind, so we didn't bother."

"Besides," Lebiya added, "it's not as if we'll be missed."

Samuel turned to face them. "I don't want you coming along if you think it's going to be some kind of adventure. This is serious. It has to do with allegiance to the God of our fathers."

"We know that."

Samuel rubbed the back of his neck. "I guess I'd become so used to traveling alone it just never occurred to me that anybody else would want to come."

"That may be true of Shemed and his brothers," Ahitub said, "but he doesn't speak for all of us. So when do we start?"

Samuel couldn't help chuckling; then he embraced each of them in turn. "You know it's going to be a long walk."

"And one I've wanted to make for a long time," Lebiya said.

"You have?"

"Ever since you returned here and told us all those stories about what happened to you there, I've wanted to see it."

"I don't think we're going to wander that far."

"Away from here is good enough for me!"

And with that said, the three of them started off in the predawn twilight.

"You didn't bring much to eat, it looks like," Ahitub said.

"I'm fasting. In fact, I haven't eaten since yesterday at sunset."

"You haven't?"

"Today—the tenth day of this month—is the Day of Atonement. It's a day set aside for afflicting our souls and turning from our sins."

"We never did anything like that before," Lebiya observed.

"I'm not surprised."

"Was this one of those things for Levites?"

"The Lord meant it for all Israel."

They said nothing else until they arrived at the crossroads, the sun just coming up behind them. The road going south led to Gibeah and Jerusalem, the one north to Mizpah.

Samuel had wondered out loud before they got there whether it would be light enough to tell the way. As it turned out it wasn't a problem, and not because of the rising sun. For the first thing they saw as they neared the crossroad was a group of a dozen people heading northward, toward Mizpah. Samuel, Lebiya, and Ahitub joined them.

"Where are you from?" Ahitub asked someone.

"From Bethlehem, in the land of the tribe of Judah," a man answered, adding, "You probably never heard of it. What about you?"

"We're from Ramah."

"Ramah! Then you must know if the seer is on his way!"

Ahitub glanced at Samuel out of the corner of his eye and smiled. "I think I can safely say that, yes, he's on the road to Mizpah at this very moment."

"Do you think we'll be able to see him?"

"He's probably not too far ahead of us."

Ahitub might have let the jest go on longer, but everyone slowed their pace. Samuel had thought that they would arrive at Mizpah early with few people waiting for him. But now that they were in sight of the towers of the city, they could see the open spaces before them covered with hundreds of people, with more arriving by the minute. Never in all his time at the sanctuary had Samuel seen so many people in one place.

Why had so many come? He didn't know whether it was because of the attack on Shiloh or the possibility that Israel was finally ready for what they had been called to do even in the wilderness: to serve the Lord and Him only. Fear and hope seemed to be the only possibilities.

The people were milling about expectantly, talking animatedly in small groups. Some discussed an imminent attack by the Sea People. Others described Samuel, whose spiritual qualities had been discernible even as a boy at Shiloh. His face burned to hear of himself spoken of in that way. Fear and hope.

"Praise the Lord you've come, Seer!"

Samuel looked around. Then he saw an old man approaching him. He recognized him as one of the elders of Mizpah, someone who spent much time at the city gate.

People now began to crowd in on Samuel from all directions, knowing that he was the seer for whom they had been waiting. Samuel had had people press in on him before, but never so many or so fervently. It was all he could do to keep from being swept off his feet. Finally he managed to start working his way toward the city gate. Stone benches lined the outer wall there, and he thought that he would have to climb up on one in order to address the mob.

Just as he reached the wall, something about the noise of the crowd changed. It started dying away sharply, replaced by a murmur that grew louder and more fearful. Samuel asked one of the elders of Mizpah what was going on.

"Our sentries on the wall have just sent word to us. Some people have just emerged over the ridge to the west. From the way they reflect the sunlight they appear to be wearing armor. It could be the Sea People!"

"How many?"

"Not too many right now. That could change, though. They were still coming up the ridge at last report."

The Sea People. That's what the people gathered here were talking about. Samuel stared to the west, but couldn't see how far away the soldiers were because of the crowd pressing around him. Perhaps he should have the people sent away, so that they could retreat to their homes . . .

No! He refused to act like a hired shepherd more worried about saving his own skin than about the sheep in his charge. God had sent him here to summon the people of Israel to trust in the Lord, and what better time to start that than now?

With a little difficulty he managed to edge closer to the bench. Just as he was about to step up onto it he recognized someone standing close by. It was the brother of Daah, looking as dark and hard as he had 10 years before. "My offer still stands," he said as he placed his hand on the hilt of his bronze knife, his expression never changing.

Samuel nodded in acknowledgment before he stepped up onto the bench. As he came into view, the people immediately surrounding him fell silent, and that silence soon spread throughout the crowd.

"This," Samuel shouted to the people, "is the day on which the Lord commanded our fathers to fast and to seek the forgiveness of God. If any here came for any other reason, leave now!" Samuel waited only a short while, but deliberately refused to survey the crowd.

Then he stepped down off the bench and turned to the city elders. "I need a small jug and also a yearling lamb. And have the men of Mizpah set up a small altar over there," he said, pointing toward the spot where Daah had been stoned to death 10 years before.

"At once, Seer."

Samuel then turned toward Daah's brother. "It looks as though I'll be taking you up on your offer. I'll be needing your knife soon."

The crowd's attention soon divided between the Sea People, who were massing in greater numbers on the western edge of the highlands, and Samuel. As the elders erected the altar, Samuel took the jug and made his way toward the nearest well. There he filled the vessel with water and returned with it to the altar—really nothing more than a small mound of piled stones. He raised the jug over his head.

"Lord," Samuel called out, "we have sinned against You. May You do this to us and more if we continue to forsake You!" With that he poured the water in the jug out over the altar. The water ran off over the stones, seeped into the ground, and disappeared.

The sight of something as precious to the highlanders as water vanishing into the ground deeply affected those who were watching. They saw themselves, both as individuals and collectively as a people, being poured out and ceasing to be. It was almost as if they could feel their lives draining away from them until their bodies were empty shells, as empty as the jug Samuel held in his hands.

Those closest to the altar immediately began to cry. Some dropped to their knees or rent their garments. Their sorrow was like a wave that washed over everyone in the crowd. People began begging the Lord for forgiveness. It wasn't a desperate sorrow in the face of a threat from God or human being. Rather, it was genuine, repentant sorrow. Samuel might have been gratified by the spectacle were he not weeping himself.

The soldiers of the Sea People were too far away to hear as they massed in the long shadow cast by the walls of Gibeah. When all the troops had assembled at the top of the ridge, they would move against Mizpah. The orders the soldiers had received were simple: break up the gathering outside Mizpah by force. No one had said anything about taking the seer prisoner. The men understood that whatever they deemed necessary—even killing him—would be sanctioned.

Samuel and the people had begun to compose themselves. The guards who remained on the city walls kept watch on the growing mass of Sea People, wondering why people weren't entering the city so that they could shut the gate.

"Bring wood for a fire," Samuel ordered. Soon they had gathered more than enough and placed it on the altar. Then Samuel had the lamb brought forward, and he borrowed the bronze knife from Daah's brother.

He had watched it being done a thousand times while he was at the sanctuary and should have been used to it, hardened to it. But in the midst of a people struggling with a mixture of sorrow and suppressed panic, with little to choose between destruction by God and destruction by human being, here huddled a wide-eyed animal that had never harmed anybody and that could have no idea what was going on. It was this knowledge that made its death the hardest thing

Samuel had ever done in his life. One second the animal was look-ing into his face, its head held up to better expose its neck. The next its knees had buckled and the light in its eyes faded the way a lamp wick dims just before going black.

Samuel held the carcass of the lamb aloft, a trail of blood cover-ing its chest. He tried to say that its death was for the sins of all Israel, but the fresh wave of wailing that rolled over the crowd drowned out his words. The lamb was placed on the altar, a flame struck, and soon the flames began to consume its body.

Weariness began to overwhelm Samuel. He was dimly aware of his own hunger, the heat of the midday sun high in a clear late-summer sky, and the continuing threat of the Sea People. Samuel felt light-headed. The clarity of vision that he had experienced when preparing to journey here now faded in the face of his own physical limitations.

"Don't stop praying for us!" someone called out from the crowd.

For the people gathered outside Mizpah, prayer no longer was something casual. It wasn't a rote speech to deliver in the presence of human beings for the benefit of the Lord. In fact, prayer wasn't words at all. Rather, it was what Moses had done in the court of Pharaoh when he demanded the freedom of Jacob's descendants. Prayer was the painting of the lamb's blood on the doorposts to avert the angel of death or Moses fasting 40 days in God's presence and receiving His law. And prayer was what pushed Eli to the edge of exhaustion year after year as he performed the rites of the Day of Atonement. Samuel had said little since his arrival at Mizpah, but he had been in almost constant prayer.

"Save us from the Sea People!" someone cried.

A great cloud of dust now began to obscure the army of Sea People as it started toward Mizpah. The guards on the wall won-dered why those outside weren't running inside. Looking toward the sky, Samuel tilted his head back and spread out his arms. He tried speaking, but got no farther than "Lord . . ."

For a few seconds Samuel said nothing. Then the silence ended.

Nobody who was there could exactly describe what happened next. That there was a sound of some sort was clear to everybody. To some it resembled thunder, but how could thunder come from a clear sky? To others it reminded them of an animal of some sort, perhaps a lion, but only a lion the size of a mountain could make a noise so deep, so unnatural. To still others it was an earthquake, but any shaking of the ground seemed to come after the noise, as if the noise had not just accompanied the tremor but had in fact caused it.

Whatever it was, only a handful of people noticed that Samuel showed no fear when it happened. In fact, his eyes were open and his mouth curved into a smile. For while everyone there heard it, only Samuel appeared to understand it.

All eyes turned to the Sea People, who had been steadily marching toward the city. Now, suddenly, discipline gave way to disorder, and a panic set in that sent them running back down toward the plains.

It didn't take long for the Israelites to realize that God had indeed delivered them. All of the pent-up emotion of the day now burst out. Men began running after the Sea People, chasing after them with whatever weapons they could pick up off the ground from where the invaders had dropped them in their flight. Soon almost half the people who had gathered around Samuel streamed westward in pursuit. Samuel felt someone grab his wrist. It was Daah's brother. Wrenching the bronze knife from Samuel's grasp, and, with a grin on his face and a cruel light in his eyes, he took off after the others. Samuel had wanted to remain at the city, but the crush of people was so great that he found himself swept along with it. He didn't manage to stop until he had reached the edge of the highlands. There people were still rushing down the foothills toward the coastal plain.

Samuel could see the white-clad Sea People fleeing across the plain toward their cities. But his heart stopped as he also saw the bodies of Sea People dotting the hills and foothills. Unused to the rough terrain and swept along in the retreat, many had fallen to their deaths.

Samuel felt his mind and heart pulled backward in time, back to Beth-Shemesh and the deaths of those who had been careless with the ark. It seemed to him that this is what they must have looked like before they had been gathered and lined up: corpses scattered across the landscape. His legs gave out under him and he sat down heavily, staring out over the land below. He stayed there until evening, when the sun began setting in the sea and coloring the landscape blood red.

★ ★ ★

Ahitub had been caught up in the emotional currents that swept over the people as Samuel had interceded for them the day before. In the same way he had found himself engulfed by the swirl of Israelites pursuing the Sea People. It was only once he was below the foothills and on the coastal plain that he could get his bearings. He, like so many others, didn't stop until they were near Ashkelon.

Turning back, the pursuers thought little of satisfying their hunger by looting the cities that the Sea People had possessed as late as that morning. Ahitub ate some bread that someone had passed to him, but hunger wasn't uppermost on his mind. He had to find Samuel and Lebiya.

That night he napped a few hours on the plain. But the experience of sleeping so close to the sea, while a novelty to him, wasn't his main concern. By the time the sun was rising in the east, he had finally found his way to the top of the ridge, and the walls of Mizpah were in sight at last.

Knots of people still clustered near the walls. Some were resting, others leisurely breaking their fast as if the events of the past day were routine. Still others talked excitedly about what had happened and compared descriptions of what they thought the noise sounded like.

As Ahitub approached the city gate, he heard a shout followed by peals of laughter. Curious, he turned to see.

A man was running out of the city, stumbling over his own feet and falling to the ground every few cubits. As he tried to get up, someone would leap up behind him and hit him across the back or in the rump with a stout piece of wood. The people at the gate seemed to think nothing of laughing at the man's misfortune. Ahitub smiled as well, but for a different reason.

"Lebiya!"

At the sound of her name the woman stopped swatting the man, who scuttled away practically on all fours. Glancing around, she saw Ahitub, ran to him, and embraced him.

"Where *were* you?" he asked.

"Here, trying to find *you!* I must've walked every cubit of this city twice! I couldn't find you anywhere, so I found someplace to sleep in a corner of a stable. Next thing I know it's morning and that . . . *fool* . . . has his hands all over me. I was just finishing up teaching him better manners when you showed up. And where have *you* been?"

"Down toward the plains. I pretty much followed the crowd down there."

"Why didn't you stay up here in the hills?"

"How could I? When everyone started chasing after the Sea People they swept everything along with them! And then I had to climb back up here. Believe me, I'm not doing *that* again any time soon! Where's Samuel?"

"I've asked around, but nobody's seen him since yesterday."

Ahitub checked with the people sitting at the gate. "Does anybody know what happened to the seer?"

A pair of old men seated at the gate spoke up. "We know."

"He went south of here," one said.

"No, he didn't; he went north!" the other contradicted.

"But that was *after* he went south!"

"Are you sure you saw him going south?"

"As sure as you are that he went north!"

"That's . . . all right," Ahitub said. "Thank you."

"So which one's right?" Lebiya asked.

"Maybe they're both right—first he went south, then he went north."

"Are you looking for the seer?" a third man at the gate asked.

"Yes," Ahitub said. "Have you seen him?"

"Not since earlier today."

"Where was he?"

"South of here, between here and Shen. I was with a group of people who followed him down there. He had us . . . well, it was strange."

"What was?"

"He had us set up a large stone. He called it the *eben ha-ezer,* the stone of help, because up until then the Lord had helped us. Then he turned and went back north. I tried to follow, but I couldn't keep up. If he's not here, he must have gone on farther north."

"Thanks," Ahitub said. "It looks as if he went farther north."

"But where would he go?" Lebiya said.

"I think I know where."

★　★　★

It was getting close to sunset when the two of them reached the end of the valley. Turning eastward, they continued walking, fighting the weariness that had plagued them all day. Lebiya had never been there before, and Ahitub only once, but he remembered it as if it had been just yesterday. If Samuel was anyplace, he was here.

Sure enough, they saw someone a ways down the valley. His donkey was tied to a small tree near the northern foothills, and he himself was seated on the ground in the middle of the valley.

"What's he. . .?" Lebiya began. Ahitub motioned that she should be quiet. The two of them approached Samuel, who took no notice of them.

"Samuel?" Ahitub asked.

"What?" His voice had something distant and lifeless about it as he sat head down.

"Samuel, what are you doing here? The Sea People have been driven away. Our people chased them as far as Beth-Car!"

The seer and judge remained silent.

"Think of what you did: you led the people of Israel to a great victory!"

"No," Samuel said as he shook his head. When he raised his head Lebiya gasped. His eyes were red from weeping and his face streaked with tears. "This was not a victory that was won by me—it was won in spite of me."

"What are you saying?" Ahitub asked. Lebiya stared at Samuel and bit her lip.

"Please, sit down. I've carried something on my heart for far too long. And I received word from the Lord yesterday that I cannot continue to serve Him until I confess."

"Confess what? You've always . . ."

"Ahitub," Lebiya said gently, "do as he says."

With that, they both sat down near him.

"It was the day that the sanctuary fell," Samuel began. "It was as if a thousand demons became unleashed when the news spread through the compound of the deaths of Eli's sons and the capture of the ark. For a long time I didn't notice what was going on. I was overcome with grief because of Eli's death, and when that was spent I buried him. Here," he said as he patted the spot of ground in front of him, "is where his body lies.

"Issachar had helped me bury Eli, and when we were finished I was about to take Issachar to Shiloh to see if I could find a new home for him. That's when I heard the crying. I followed it to one of the few tents still standing. It was Phinehas's tent.

"There was nobody inside except a baby—a boy. He looked as if he'd just been born: he was naked and unwashed; his navel string had not been cut. While I knew that Phinehas's wife was expecting a child, I wasn't aware that she had gone into labor.

"I looked outside and called to the few people who had yet to run away. Nobody seemed to listen. Finally I found one of the Levites. I asked him who the child was. 'They named him Ichabod ["the glory has departed"],' he told me. 'Where is his mother?' I asked. 'Dead,' he said. 'They took her body away when they left.' Then he fled as well.

"I don't know what made me do it, but I wrapped the baby up in some clothing that I found in the tent and took him with me. Issachar called me a fool all the way to Shiloh. 'That name is his legacy,' he kept insisting. 'Let him die with it in peace.' But I wouldn't listen. After asking the potter in Shiloh to take on Issachar and to give him shelter, I started for home.

"I don't remember much of anything after leaving Shiloh. Everything that happened—the fall of the sanctuary, the death of Eli and his sons—it all overwhelmed me, and I couldn't focus on what was happening. All I know is that somehow I made it home."

Stunned, Ahitub suddenly began to sense where Samuel's story was headed.

"Hannah had been pregnant and had also gone into labor on the day the sanctuary fell," Lebiya added. "Waking wide-eyed and sweating that morning, she started to speak of a dream that she'd had; then her labor pains overtook her. Almost everybody was out in the field working, and I had to help deliver the child all by myself. Hannah gave birth to a son, but . . . but it was born dead.

"Just then Elkanah entered the house, his arm around Samuel, holding him up to keep him from collapsing. We saw that Samuel was carrying an infant at the same time Elkanah realized that his new son was dead.

"I'm not surprised that Samuel doesn't remember what happened then. He was completely exhausted and fell to the floor unconscious. While Elkanah laid Samuel down and made him comfortable, Hannah and I looked at each other and then at the infant. Without saying a word, we all agreed on what we would do. We placed the body of the stillborn in a jar and buried it in a grove of trees, and Hannah accepted the infant Samuel had brought home in place of the son she had lost. It was Samuel who circumcised the boy when he was eight days old, and it was Samuel who had already thought of a new name for him."

Ahitub looked up. "A new name," he said as if in a daze, "my name. Who else knew about this?"

"Hannah, Elkanah, Samuel, and I. The others never knew what had happened. Shemed and his brothers probably wouldn't have cared one way or the other even if they had known."

"But why wasn't I told sooner?"

"I'm sorry," Samuel said, tears filling his eyes again. "I didn't want you to know."

"You *what!*"

"Your father was one of the sons of Eli killed in the battle at Aphek, when the Sea People took the ark captive. Even before that he was . . ."

"I don't care what he was—he was my *father!*"

"Well, you *should* care! It was because of him that Israel lost the ark and the sanctuary . . . well, look around you! Nothing is left of it, nothing! That's your father's legacy to Israel, and it didn't stop there. The Levites of Beth-Shemesh—they didn't know any better, and look what happened to them: 70 dead in one day! The whole Levitical priesthood had become compromised, corrupted. It deserved to be swept away!"

"But it wasn't," Lebiya interrupted. "Thanks to you."

"What are you talking about?"

"You constantly speak against the Levites and the sons of Eli. But you saved the life of one of them. Rescued the grandson of Eli, a direct descendant of the high priest. He's sitting right here in front of you. Why?"

Samuel paused, looking from Lebiya to Ahitub and back again. His anger at the sons of Eli, which he had carried in his heart since the days of the tabernacle, had been pounding in his ears as he had shouted against them just now. But now as he looked into the face of the young man seated before him, a face very much like his father's, yet gentler and more peaceful, the anger inside him burned away like morning fog. "I don't know why," he said in a voice that was exhausted, dead.

"I do," Ahitub said quietly. "I remember what you told someone once in Bethel: there is no greater obligation laid on anyone than to save a life."

Samuel was silent for a moment; then he threw himself across the ground and wept more bitterly than he had before. Ahitub and Lebiya watched in silence. Gradually Samuel's groans and sobs became more coherent and began to form words: "I'm sorry, Eli! I couldn't save you! I'm sorry!"

It was some time before Samuel's grief was exhausted. Ahitub and Lebiya wept as well—Ahitub with his face buried in his hands rocking back and forth, Lebiya in silence.

"You did save him," Lebiya said at last. "You saved his grandson. That's enough."

"Samuel," Ahitub said as he took his foster brother by the arms and sat him up, "what was he like?"

"Your father, Phinehas?"

"No. My grandfather Eli. Was he a good man?"

"I think his heart was good but his spirit was weak. I saw him only when he was old, when his two sons had had their way for so long that there was barely enough strength in him to get through one day and to wait for the next. But there were times . . . there were times when I thought I could see what he used to be. I thought I could see some light in his eyes."

"I wouldn't be surprised if he got some of that light from you," Lebiya said. Samuel's face flushed. "If this was where the ark once stood," she went on, "that means you must have slept right around here somewhere."

"Yes," Samuel said, standing, "yes, it must have been . . . right about . . . here. This must be where the menorah once stood. I used to sleep just below it when I was little."

"What was that like?" Ahitub asked.

Samuel hesitated.

"He's entitled to know, Samuel," Lebiya said. "Now more than ever."

"I don't know that I can . . . it's been so long . . ."

"You used to be such a good storyteller," she teased. "Don't tell me you've stopped just because you've become a seer."

"No, it's . . . it's just that . . . I was wondering whether we shouldn't be getting back to Ramah."

"Why? So we can watch Shemed play with his iron toy?"

For long into that night, as a fire burned and the three of them cooked and divided a handful of provisions, Samuel pulled out of his heart every memory he could about Eli, the sanctuary, the garrulous old Levite who became a potter, and about the young novice who had been a friend—about people and places and things once feared or cherished but now all vanished.

"Samuel," Ahitub asked at one point, "did you really mean it when you said that the Levites were all corrupted?"

"I meant it when I said it, because I believed it after seeing what I did when I was here. I don't know that I feel that way now, though."

"Because of me?"

"Because even if they did forget the Lord and His law—even if they did become corrupt in His service here—God still set aside the tribe of Levi for His service and to enact the rites in His law. May the Lord forgive my hatred!"

"It's not as if you didn't have your reasons," Lebiya commented.

"What happens now?" Ahitub asked.

"We go home in the morning, I guess," she replied.

"No, Lebiya, what happens after that? I'm a Levite, and I'm not saying that because I want to be treated different or anything. But it has to mean something."

"The Levites have no land, you know that," Samuel said.

"It's not about land—you're starting to sound like Shemed. It's about who my kinspeople are, and whether there are any left."

"Why can't you simply stay at Ramah?"

"Maybe I will. Or maybe I won't—I don't know."

"If you were to leave," Lebiya said, "Hannah would miss you. And Elkanah."

"I know."

"Now, if Peninah were still alive . . ."

After a moment of silence the three of them burst out laughing. Each of them knew only too well what Peninah had been like. None of them needed to say anything further. It was the perfect family joke.

"What *is* going to happen?" Ahitub repeated as the laughter died down.

"I don't know," Samuel replied as he shook his head. "Even though I'm a seer I just don't know."

★   ★   ★

The news of Ahitub's true parentage caused no real surprise in the household of Elkanah. Ahitub was huskier than any of the other men in the family, so that actually served to clear up what some had thought to be a mystery.

Of far greater news was the account of what had happened at Mizpah. Elkanah and those of his family who had remained at Ramah had already heard several versions of the incident. That of Samuel, Ahitub, and Lebiya was no less fantastic for being true.

Nobody directly accused Shemed of collaborating with the Sea People, though when asked about the circumstances under which he had once again acquired an iron plowshare he became sullen and uncommunicative. Samuel never questioned him about it, which upset him all the more.

★   ★   ★

They arrived one day during the winter, when the rains were at their heaviest and nobody would be out on the roads unless they had a compelling reason.

But their visit was not unexpected. Samuel had been making

frequent journeys throughout Benjaminite territory and even beyond all through the fall months. Shemed had muttered more than
once—in a tone that he meant to be heard—that Samuel was once
more avoiding his responsibilities around the farm, but even his own
full brothers did not respond to what he said this time, let alone the
children of Hannah. The family gathered in the harvest with a sullen
silence that hung over them like a cloud.

Then, just before the onset of winter, Samuel's search and in-
quiries bore fruit. In Nob, a settlement just north of Jerusalem, he
found an old man named Asarel whose daughter had been the wife
of Phinehas and the mother of Ichabod. When Samuel told him that
his daughter's child was alive and living in Ramah, Asarel had said
nothing. Finally he agreed to visit Samuel in Ramah "when I can get
there." He did not show up until winter.

Two men about the age of Elkanah accompanied him. All three
of them seemed to Samuel as hard as flint.

"Why couldn't Ahitub have gone to them instead?" Izhar asked
under his breath. "Especially on a day like this!"

"What's the matter?" Lebiya retorted, her voice low as well.
"Afraid they'll eat the food out of your bowl?"

Izhar started to reply, but before he could say anything a fat drop
of rainwater dripped from the roof and landed right between his
eyes. Shaking his head and snorting like an ox, he moved away as his
sister fought back the urge to laugh.

Samuel and Lebiya repeated for Asarel how Samuel had rescued
the child from the sanctuary at Shiloh and raised him in the household of Elkanah. Asarel said nothing for a while as he stared at
Ahitub. The look in his eyes never softened.

"You have your mother's features, I'll grant you that," he said
at length. "Or what I remember of them. Didn't he have any
other children?"

The man's comment took Samuel by surprise. When he had spoken to Asarel before, the old man had never brought up the matter.

"There was another boy," Ahitub suddenly answered. "Named
Ichabod. He died after he was born."

"Just as well," his grandfather replied. "Can't see anyone drag-
ging that name around with them all their life. So," he continued,

his voice stronger, less distant, "think they can spare you here? Looks as if they've got enough to keep the farmstead going without you."

Everyone looked toward Ahitub—everyone except Samuel, who gazed at the floor. Ahitub did not say anything for a while. "May I give you my answer in the morning?"

Shemed and Izhar exchanged disapproving glances. Having had their fill of strangers, they did not like the idea of the three visitors staying the night.

Asarel nodded, and Hannah began making accommodations for them. As for Samuel, he walked out the door, Ahitub following closely behind him. The two of them walked to the nearby sheep-fold in the courtyard, which had a primitive roof to provide the animals some protection. It offered enough room for the two to stand together underneath it.

"And what is your answer?" Samuel demanded, looking straight ahead of him at the winter rain.

"I . . . I want you to understand . . ."

"I do understand. You've given me your answer."

"Then why are you acting as if I'm dead or something?"

"I . . . I don't know," Samuel said wearily as he brushed his hair, wet from the rain, from his eyes. "I know you don't belong here, not really. That's why I went looking for your family, to see if anyone still survived."

"And you've never felt that way yourself?"

"What way?"

"That you don't belong here?"

Samuel paused, glanced at Ahitub, and managed a faint smile. "Maybe you *do* understand. Ahitub, when I first came back here after Eli died, I wanted to feel as if I did belong here, but I didn't. I never have. The tabernacle was the only home I ever knew, and when that was gone . . ." He again wiped the winter rain from his face. "Ahitub, I helped raise you all those years after the tabernacle fell. You were like a living part of it."

"Because Eli was my grandfather."

Samuel nodded.

"I wish I could feel the same way, Samuel, but I honestly can't. I never knew Eli, except from the stories you've told me. And now

I'm supposed to be part of a family I've never known. I'm supposed to make a life with a people I've never met—like Asarel. But why can't this be my family?" he protested. "You and Lebiya and Hannah and everyone?"

"Even Shemed?"

Ahitub thought a long time, then slowly wilted like a flower in the summer sun. "It still feels wrong to have to choose," he finally said.

"I know," Samuel answered gently. "This is a lot harder than any decision I've ever had to render as a judge."

"What should I do?" Ahitub said as he grasped Samuel's arm. "I know what I'm *supposed* to do, but isn't there some other way?"

With a sigh Samuel looked the other way. "Don't ask me. I'm only a seer."

Then before Ahitub could say another word, Samuel walked back into the house.

★   ★   ★

The following spring, during the barley harvest, Ahitub announced to the family that he was leaving Ramah. When Samuel heard of the decision he left the room and barely said two words to him after that. Elkanah tried to get Samuel to explain himself, but Ahitub and Lebiya discouraged him from prying. So did Hannah.

Ahitub left on a day when the latter rains of spring had let up. Because he was a Levite he made no claim on a share of an inheritance from Elkanah, but the family gave him enough that, by dint of trading, he acquired a donkey to carry what possessions he could claim as his own. As he tied things onto the animal's back Elkanah and several others—people who not so long ago he would have claimed as his own family—silently and sadly watched him.

"You'll let us know how you're doing," Hannah said.

"Of course I will. Where's . . . ?"

"Still inside," Lebiya said. "He wouldn't say anything when I told you were getting ready to leave."

Ahitub glanced over at the field where some of the others were at work. "Say goodbye to Shemed and Izhar and the others for me." Then, hugging Elkanah, Hannah, and Lebiya, he turned to leave.

"Wait!"

Samuel stood in the doorway. Stepping outside, he handed a cloth bundle to Ahitub.

"This isn't big enough for you to wear," he said, "but . . . I thought you should have this."

"Should I open it?"

"I don't see why not."

The bundle contained clothes, small garments that would fit a boy about 12 years of age: a long blue robe, a short embroidered sleeveless coat, a matching belt, a turban, and a linen garment with two leg holes and a drawstring.

"There was a linen robe, but it was in pretty bad shape by the time I arrived home. It got cut up and used for other things long ago."

Ahitub looked up. "Why?"

"I didn't think that the Levites would ever serve in the sanctuary again. All right, I didn't *want* to see the Levites resume their roles. But maybe the Lord will cause the sanctuary to be rebuilt in some form or other. And I thought that one of the Levites should at least have a model for the vestments of the high priest. Even if he can't wear them himself," he added with a smile.

"You've given me more than enough already. You have truly lived the name you gave me—Ahitub, 'a good brother.'"

Samuel and Ahitub held each other close. Lebiya couldn't help noticing Samuel's shoulders trembling slightly. Ahitub then turned and led the donkey out of the courtyard and toward the road that would take him toward the people who were his family and his fellow tribespeople and away from those who had cared for him.